like animals

like animals

A NOVEL

Eve LemiEUx

TRANSLATED BY CAYMAN ROCK

RARE
MACHINES

Publisher: Scott Fraser | Acquiring editor: Russell Smith
Cover designer: Michel Vrana | Cover image: istock.com/SaulHerrera

Library and Archives Canada Cataloguing in Publication

Title: Like animals : a novel / Eve Lemieux ; translated by Cayman Rock.
Other titles: Comme des animaux. English
Names: Lemieux, Eve, 1990- author.
Description: Translation of: Comme des animaux.
Identifiers: Canadiana (print) 20210291753 | Canadiana (ebook) 2021029194X | ISBN 9781459747821 (softcover) | ISBN 9781459747838 (PDF) | ISBN 9781459747845 (EPUB)
Classification: LCC PS8623.E54232 C6613 2022 | DDC C843/.6—dc23

We acknowledge the support of the Canada Council for the Arts and the Ontario Arts Council for our publishing program. We also acknowledge the financial support of the Government of Ontario, through the Ontario Book Publishing Tax Credit and Ontario Creates, and the Government of Canada.

This translation was made possible by the financial support of Société de développement des entreprises culturelles.

Care has been taken to trace the ownership of copyright material used in this book. The author and the publisher welcome any information enabling them to rectify any references or credits in subsequent editions.

The publisher is not responsible for websites or their content unless they are owned by the publisher.

Printed and bound in Canada.

Rare Machines, an imprint of Dundurn Press
1382 Queen Street East
Toronto, Ontario, Canada M4L 1C9
dundurn.com, @dundurnpress

For Virg and Mat, my two true loves.

all too human
this breathing
in and out
out and in
these punks
these cowards
these champions
these mad dogs of glory
moving this little bit of light toward us
impossibly

— Charles Bukowski,
"Beasts Bounding Through Time"

Prologue

Death Mask of a Young Woman

The sun rises lazily over the horizon. Stretching endlessly into the distance, the sea calls to me. We sip our coffees next to the ocean at low tide, our feet in a little muddy hole. A thousand cotton candy clouds tickle the sky with ghostly fingers, and a white tern splits the air with its cry. It beats its wings fiercely on the horizon and rides the winds — totally free. "Stay with me, free bird," I want to yell, but my lips refuse to open.

Raphael is already heading back to the cottage to start a fire on yesterday's ashes and set a lovely breakfast table, whistling while he cooks. Idiot. He gets on my nerves with his cheeriness, his positive, unflappable demeanour. His goddamn breathing. And his *fucking* hiking shoes. I'm going to slash them to ribbons with a steak knife, him and his disgusting Salomons. Saved by the bell: he closes the toilet door, settling in for his morning dump. Shit out of luck. I lose myself looking back at the horizon, wishing I could pull it over me like a blanket.

The words to "Shine On You Crazy Diamond" trickle through my mind.

Sitting atop a coconut-shaped boulder, Tania lights a menthol bitch stick. Even with her face all smudged with a hangover, my best friend is still beautiful. Cuddling next to her is like clutching my blankie.

Why do I feel like I'm just an extra in this movie?

Louis, naked and dishevelled, steps out of his tent, already making fun of his own raspy voice. Daniel, who has been pissing on a bush, tackles him, and they start rolling over and over one another. They wrestle in brotherly fashion, in the buff. Raphael, not one to miss out, leaps out from the toilet to join the limp dick–pissing contest. They laugh like kids, yell their lungs out, push and pull while completely ignoring my look of contempt.

"Fucking idiots," Tania puffs.

Her cigarette smoke makes me gag. I walk up the bank with heavy feet while kicking every rock and piece of driftwood I come across. I'm the lead martyr in the cautionary tale of my own invention.

The wind picks up while Raphael starts setting the wooden table with cutely mismatched placemats and patterned napkins. Birthday decorations worthy of the glossiest magazines. My heart braces for an attack.

Daniel finally has his shorts on and steps out of the cottage, hands full of local, organic, sustainable produce — the whole deal. Nausea hits me again. Tania walks up to him, gliding her hand over his crotch and biting his earlobe. Raphael apes their eroticism by coming up to me holding an enormous strawberry that he wants to watch me eat like a little kitty cat. "Fuck off, I'm not your pet," I wish I could say as I sink my teeth into the berry. Juicy and sweet. He smiles, contented by our low-key happiness, our undeniable bond. He makes me eat out of his hand; that must be it — the recipe for a happy couple. Bacon and sausages that need attention finally make him leave me alone.

"You going to help me with the omelette, Louis? The rest of you, help yourselves to the pastries while you wait. It's going to be a helluva brunch, peeps."

Brunch. Brunch is supposed to be on a noisy patio with bottomless mimosas sometime after noon, wearing a thin dress and a perverted smile, being waited on by a waiter while chit-chatting, our responsibilities shelved sometime between the previous night's last shot and the latest morning fuck. It isn't even eight o'clock, and I want to set the world on fire.

A flock of seagulls cry their lungs out above the sea. Being born in a human body is fucking shit.

Tania and Daniel suck face in the otherwise empty bay. Those two are insatiable. They fuck like animals all day and night, scream at each other like banshees, and hurl the most terrible insults I've ever heard at each other. Sometimes other things get thrown. I can still remember the time when Tania, drunk off her ass, caught him flirting with the downstairs neighbour. "I was just asking for some eggs, you crazy bitch." But Tania isn't stupid. She knows no one makes an omelette, pancakes, or a fucking cake at three in the morning. The eggs exploded on the neighbour's window, and the girl went back into her apartment with a bloody nose. Daniel and Tania punched and kicked, tore at each other's hair, bit until they drew blood in the fire escape. The "fucking douche" and the "fucking bitch" shouted their faces off until the cop sirens froze them in their tracks. They were going to break up that time, for sure. But Tania told me how after they left the police station they buried the hatchet in La Belle Province's filthy toilet stall.

I can't even recognize myself in the mirror. I've brainwashed myself into a romantic coma. We used to be crazy in love, too. Alive. This wasn't the plan, babe. No way. We were supposed to shine like motherfucking diamonds while the rest of the world watched, not keep up this hypocritical act, separated by the crush of normality. No fucking way. What happened to my fire, my fury, my spark? My life is bullshit. But so is yours, you fucking asshole.

"Louis! Daniel! Would you guys give me a hand?"

Raphael taps his feet on the steps, looking *fabulous* in his flowery apron. Louis separates the couple mid-French and yanks Daniel by the neck all the way back to the cottage. Happy to finally get some attention, Raphael whips their asses with a dishcloth. While the three Gordon Ramsays finish fussing over my birthday meal, I can feel myself sleepwalking toward a minefield.

1

Villeray, January 2016

Cars and buses struggle, beached in banks of snow. You can only get around on foot if you're properly equipped. The storm has the entire city stunned, but nothing can stop Tania and me. We climb great piles of the stuff, dodge the plows, and build snowmen with cigarette noses. We're twenty-five, going on twelve.

The snow floats down from the sky like in a rom-com. I've only ever known one truly happy couple.

"How are your parents doing, Tan?"

She takes a long drag on her menthol. My eyes drift up toward a lamppost; it won't hurt so bad if I don't look directly at her.

"The house I grew up in … they actually sold it."

"Huh?"

"Sylvain went back to Marseille."

"What the fuck! No way. What's your mom going to do?"

"Same as usual. She'll become a workaholic and then burn herself out. Louis and me offered to help her move, but she basically told us to fuck off. Guess she'll be fucking alone, then."

Tania Reynier: cold and hard as ice. My best friend.

Her parents, Manon and Sylvain, have been my model couple since I was five. The only couple that ever seemed real because their imperfections were … perfect. They were always arguing, but every night they would end up cuddling on the sofa or laughing too loud on the balcony. It seemed simple and safe. And now it's over.

"Think he found someone else?"

"I think he needs to find *himself*, you know?"

"No. I don't get it … freaks me out."

"You're scared?"

"Are you going to leave me, too?"

"Come on, Philly."

"Promise me that we'll end up like your mom's aunties in her wedding pics: still cute, just a little wrinkly, drinking champagne in little pastel dresses. Just promise me we'll always be a team."

"You got it."

It's weird that you know my parent's wedding album by heart. You looked through it how many times while we waited for supper to be served? Louis and I would watch Radio Enfer *after playing outside all day. You'd automatically take out the album and let the mint green sofa swallow you up. It was lame how you would rather look at an old wedding dress than watch Carl the Cat's killer smile on the TV. Every time, you'd say that you'll have an album just like that one day ... cream with gold accents. It always sucked because I thought it was dumb as shit. When my dad would yell at us to "turn off the goddamn TV" and come to supper, it was like a slinky bounced us right up to the table. You, you had to take the time to put the album back in exactly the right place on the bookshelf, or you'd spaz right out. You were always the last to come to the table, but Sylvain never yelled at you, Silly-Philly. It, like, pissed me off.*

The Deli Plus shines like an oasis in a bleached desert. Tania and me shamelessly dig into our poutine with extra bacon, garlic bread on the side.

Two drunk guys walk in, laughing. I sit a little straighter without even realizing what I'm doing. Either because we look cute, cheeks pink from the cold, or because they're dripping with testosterone, they sit down with us without even asking. They start chatting us up like we've been friends forever. Their blind arrogance is actually fun; we don't normally talk politics, movies, and hard drugs with a fledgling douchebag accountant and a Colombian filmmaker.

One of them is called Daniel Torrès. He invites us back to his place for a beer. Not sure I want to. I'm starting to get tired. I want to take a bath ... but, Thelma never leaves her Louise behind. Best friends forever.

At the corner of rue L.-O.-David and des Écores, reality catches up to me like a bitch in heat. The ratty old army jacket stinks of sweat under my winter coat. What am I doing, going to an apartment with two guys I don't even know, dressed like a goddamn hobo, something like forty-five minutes from our place? I feel doubt growing in my belly. Tania is walking with Daniel fucking far ahead of me, I'm pissed, muttering under by breath, and sweat is pouring down my back.

"Don't walk fast, do you, girly?"

This, from the other guy, the one with a chiselled jaw and ocean-blue eyes. His likes, off the cuff: *Pulp Fiction*, Red Hot Chili Peppers, and Emma Watson. Of course. A BMX accident blew both his knees when he was fourteen. Enjoys a little salvia from time to time. Only child, like me, only he's already been blown by twin sisters and doesn't like tomatoes. Not interested at all. Nope. Nope. Nope.

"My legs feel like Jell-O, my feet are frozen, you said it'd take fifteen minutes, and we've been walking since forever. I fucking quit."

"Want me to carry you?"

"No. Thanks. I'm no princess."

I refuse the smoke that he offers. Because I don't want my lips to touch the filter where his have been. And, more importantly, I won't start smoking again. Not for this guy. He says he's thinking of quitting himself and asks me how I managed.

"My dad's got lung cancer."

"Oh shit."

A few metres ahead of us, Daniel and Tania are climbing the stairs outside a triplex.

The guys have a beer pong table set up in the kitchen. Only wannabe alcoholics play beer pong, but I let myself get carried away by Tania's excitement. I'm the first to take off my sweater, playing in my bra, hair full of beer, cheeks on fire. I share a secret smile with my new beer pong partner, Jeffrey Hudon, finance major, chain-smoker, arrogant, and sexy, Daniel's roommate since he started university.

We're beating Daniel and Tania five to three. They suggest we smoke a joint. Our silence is thick with subtext. Tania can't help but shoot me a wink before going out on the balcony. To encourage me? To reassure me?

Jeff offers me a big T-shirt and a glass of wine that we drink sitting cross-legged on his bed. The floor is carpeted with discarded clothes; math formulae and graphs are taped artlessly on the walls. My fingers draw an imaginary wonderland on the window frost.

"You and Tania, you've been friends your whole lives, that it?"

"Yeah. How did you and Daniel meet?"

"Kijiji. Was looking for an apartment."

"Hm. And found true love."

"You're a funny one, girly. I like that, a witty girl."

It isn't funny. It's a game. I know the rules *cold*. And I can spot losers from miles away. When I find a player who makes me want to break the rules, I start playing the *real* game.

"You play sports?"

"When I was a teenager, I swam competitively, but I quit."

"Why?"

"I had no tits, no periods, and no life. I didn't want to miss out on smoking joints in the school yard on Friday nights anymore."

"Typical private school girl."

"You? Baseball, basketball … curling?"

"Nope. I go to the gym … sometimes."

"Typical douche."

"Not shy, are you?"

"Not really, nope."

"What do you do, for work?"

"Beautician."

"Fancy! Actors, models?"

"Nah. Dead people."

"You're kidding."

"No joke."

"You put makeup on dead bodies?"

"Yup."

"Shit. You're a brave one."

"What are you talking about? They're dead. They can't hurt me or rape me. If you can trust anyone, it's dead people."

"Fair enough."

He crosses his arms behind his head and leans against the bare pillows. His biceps look like two hills I want to climb. Can't say I don't like a real, living man's warm skin. I throw back the corner store Cabernet and try to escape the mattress that's pulling me down. My walls are crumbling, I have to get out of here, need to get moving. I put both hands on the bed so I don't crumple in on myself. His warm breath wafts over to me when he says, "Leaving already?"

"Uh-huh."

"You're too drunk to walk, girly."

"Tania'll walk with me ... I'm fine ..."

I open the door to see Daniel with Tania's nipples in his mouth while she jerks him off with both hands. The door slams shut.

"Oh my god. I just saw your roommate's cock."

I laugh, but I'm crying on the inside because I'm slowly losing my best friend to a massive dick.

The rough winter wind whips my face. Jeffrey smokes out the open window, his hand reaching into the cold.

"Hey. You slept like a baby, girly."

"I think ... did I fall asleep ..."

"Mid-sentence? Yeah."

"Sorry."

"No prob. It was cute."

Okay. I have to leave. Now. My tights are lost somewhere in the sheets, and my panties are digging into my crack.

"Want to give me your number? In case you get stuck in a snowbank ... that would suck."

We trade numbers like it's no big deal ... except a thousand butterflies are bouncing around inside my stomach. If I don't get out right now, he's going to kiss me, and I'm never going to leave.

Tania is touching up her nail polish on the side of the bathtub I've been soaking in for way too long.

"It was crazy, Philly. I've never seen one so big, so beautiful."

"I know. I saw it, too, actually."

"You should have felt how hard it got …"

"No, thanks, thanks."

" … big and veiny as hell. I've never pulled off a deep throat so good, and you know how hard I try."

"Uh-huh."

"How about you?"

"What about me?"

"The roommate, duh!"

"What about the roommate?"

"Did you guys fuck?"

"No. I fell asleep."

"Philly!"

"I don't even know the guy. And he's a douchebag, too."

"So? You were clicking during beer pong …"

"That's because I hate losing, and he was better than your Daniel."

"Oh my god, Daniel. My own angel, Daniel."

The bubbles in the tub pop silently while Tania goes on and on about how well Daniel ate her ass. The conversation is sinking down the tub's drain. Jeffrey. He smelled like spicy co-logne and cigarette smoke. Crazy that I like that so much. His big strong hands stung mine with every victory high-five, his mocking smile tickling my stomach. That overpowering alpha male attitude makes me melt. Maybe I should call him? See him again and try not to fall asleep this time. No. Fuck, no. I don't need that shit anymore, guys like that, who bowl me over and rip out my insides.

I can still remember Martin, fucking asshole with a nose like a pickaxe, who fucked every girl in town but promised me, me, innocent little me, that I was so special, so different, so lovable, that I would be his wife, the one and only *Mrs.* Martin. I invested heart and soul in our relationship and found myself naked in the middle of a battlefield, defending our pa-thetic love story all by myself. Angry, cheated, crazy when he became my enemy, I pushed him to the edge and beyond. And he gave up. When he left me, I whored myself out completely. I can't remember how many nights I walked back and forth in front of his favourite bar like a stupid ex with no self-esteem. Or how many times I took the 45 Papineau in the hopes of running into him, sitting next to him, taking a spontaneous walk together that, I had to believe, would eventually lead back to his bed. I texted him all the time without ever getting an answer. I followed him around the university and pretended to run into him by chance, stalked his Facebook every half hour, kept talking to his friends to stay part of the group, all for nothing. Martin didn't want me anymore.

After weeks of rage, anger and dreams of revenge replaced the hurt. Those dreams were so *real* that I sometimes had a hard time telling them from being awake. Did I slash his bike tires in real life? Or just in my dreams? Did I send his mom a positive pregnancy test in the mail? I think so. But what I *am* sure of is one night I turned down the cute guy who worked at the Uni bookstore, who had worked up the courage to ask me out. No way I would try being happy with someone else. And when I got an abortion alone on a Wednesday afternoon, Martin didn't come to my bedside to tell me that he had made a mistake and that he still loved me. Instead, he was in a cottage on Lake Brome doing coke off some bitch's ass.

True love may still exist, but it's left a bitter aftertaste in the back of my throat. So, Jeffrey-the-roommate, fuck that.

I love you, Tania, but I don't have the strength to share in your excitement. My head slips under the water, and the conversation goes over my head.

2

Argentina, August 2008

The Córdoba sun hangs like a big blood orange. It's almost seven o'clock. The plane door opens and gives you an unforgettable view of emptiness below. It's almost time to jump. I swear, we'll never forget this trip for the rest of our lives.

It's taking forever.

Ten thousand feet between your toes and the ground, but I can feel your nervousness like the wind howling in my face. Time to fly through the sky, bestie. You can do it, come on, don't chicken out. Vertigo gripping your stomach tight? That's normal.

"Jump, Philly!"

We didn't come all this way for nothing.

Now, you're falling. Must be yelling as loud as you can, but I can't hear a thing. The wind is so strong that the skin is pulling away from your face. I know — my face looks like that, too. You're free, my best friend.

We float back down to Earth softly, smoothly. You're so excited that your eyes are popping out of your head.

"We made it, Tania. You see? I did it."

Hell, yes, I saw you. I couldn't even blink.

Vodka Red Bulls to celebrate in a club packed with young tourists who all look like us, except that we, we're at the top of our game. Our little dresses rub up against faceless shirts; our hair, wet with sweat, clinging to other faces … hands move up and down your body. You look like a baby being held for the first time. Eighteen and finally free.

Swallowed by a kissing crowd, you give me silent permission to go have a smoke on the terrace. You're in good hands, and I've earned myself a minute to rest. I don't get to finish my smoke: you climb onto the roof of the club, grabbing a pair of muscular arms. Your leg is bleeding. You must have slipped.

You look so cute when you're on the prowl.

He rubs his hands together and warms your ankle. Looks like it's doing the trick.

"Are you okay, Philly?"

Your face screams that you're better than okay. You're in heaven. Finally, you're going to lose your virginity to an Irish boy with blue-grey eyes, a light tan, and a red beard, just like you always wanted.

So, you don't need me to watch out for you, anymore … it's like you have a little wing poking out of your shoulder blade. You leave without realizing that I'm making out with some hobbit. I wish someone would save me, *sometimes.*

The night flies by without you. I keep telling myself … you're doing it! My bestie is getting lucky. At least your first time isn't going to be in the back of a car with a virgin who can't get a condom on.

Dawn rises like a shining asshole. But … if the guy is a … should I call … the … cops? I don't worry long because, you know, tequila knocks me right out.

Quarter to noon. You burst into the dorm looking like a red-faced raccoon.

"Damn. Good thing you showed up, I was getting ready to call the cops."

You shove your face into a pillow and howl like an animal.

"What the hell?"

You scream and spit and punch the mattress, anything to keep yourself from crying.

"My god, Philly, what's wrong with you?"

"I lost my virginity to a freak."

"What?"

"Eamonn, the fucking beautiful guy from the bar, is a sex addict, Tania. He spanked my ass so hard I could have sworn that I was going to cry. But guess what? I loved it. He made me love it, the psycho."

"But … just because he likes it rough doesn't mean he's a pervert —"

"Wait, I'm not finished. After, we light up a jay, we talk, you know, chill … I try to look relaxed even though my pussy hurts *like fuck. Then, he tells me that he's on an abstinence retreat. That he's hiking the Andes to 'free himself' but that I made him fall off the wagon. GODDAMN IT. The guy's obsessed, Tania. He'll fuck anyone, anytime, and he gets off on keeping a log of his lays in a notebook. A goddamn fucking notebook."*

"Okay. Wow. That's really gross."

"But, the worst thing in all this — it gets worse — is that he's married, Tania."

"Oh no ... poor her."

"I just ended their marriage! It's my fault if they get divorced — because of me that he relapsed ... "

"Hey, hey, hey, it's not your fault, Philly. The guy was in a bar at three in the morning. What do you think he was doing there?"

"Am I a slut?"

"No! You didn't know that he was married, before sleeping with him ... "

You lay your head on my knees, your cries soften. You almost purr, "Think I should friend him on Facebook?"

Did you really not know, Philly?

3

Somewhere in Hell, Halloween 2012

Black eyeliner, huge gold hoops in my ears, an ebony wig that falls along my jawline. I, Cleopatra Flynn, rabid sex kitten, walk up Mont-Royal pouring a bottle of bubbly right down my throat.

Step into the bar. Shot, dance, shot, puff of weed, shot, throw up, dance, line of coke.

"I'M SO FUCKING BORED! WHAT THE HELL!"

Another bar, Jägerbomb mouthwash, grind my ass on a rapper dressed up as a pimp.

Fuck, yeah.

Smoke a gigantic joint in his car, suck him off out of courtesy, throw up in the glovebox. Almost get hit by a car crossing the street, tell the driver to go fuck himself, bum a cigarette from a girl dressed as a unicorn, make out with unicorn, smoke a king size, throw up. Walk barefoot up the sidewalk, makeup melting down my cheeks, stop in front of his apartment. Climb the fire escape, break the kitchen window, slide across the glass-covered counter, hand covered in blood. Wrap a dishcloth around my hand, find the roommate's painkillers, swallow the whole thing with some leftover mouldy wine. Collapse in Martin's living room in the hope that he'll find me and make everything better.

I wake up in the emergency room.

My breath reeks, and I'm having my period all over my green hospital gown. An enormous nurse adjusts my fluids and tells me that I'll have to meet with a shrink before I can be released.

"Can I have a pad or a tampon?"

She hands me a diaper. My stomach burns with shame.

Red hair bounces along the hall. Tania, my best friend, is looking for me. Tania, I'm sorry, I'm exhausted. I'm a hot mess, Tania. She's fucking pissed, her eyes glowing with unshed tears. She doesn't say anything and it's scary.

I had prepared a blistering speech to tell you just how scared I was that I was going to lose you. To tell you how selfish it is to go and kill yourself over some dumb fucking guy when we're right here. Well, I'm right here. I love you … but you're fucking breaking my heart. You look … you look like a little chicken ready to be slaughtered. Goddamn it, Philly … I told you to come over when you feel like that. Even that asshole, Martin, I'm the one he fucking called when he found you.

Tania throws herself across me and squeezes me hard. It's awkward but almost feels nice.

4

No more trying to get in touch with Martin. It's a matter of life or death, apparently. Block him on Facebook, unfriend all his friends, and finally delete my own account because there's always a way to find someone you shouldn't be looking for in the first place. But that isn't enough. The whole city smells like Martin. No more hanging out in the Latin Quarter; I'm going to live with my dad on boulevard Roland-Therrien.

His one-bedroom has no decorations except a Brigitte Bardot poster stuck to the wall above the couch I'll be crashing on. Dad works in a textile factory. He smokes a carton a week and hacks, coughs, and spits all the time. But he welcomes me into his apartment without judging or asking me any questions. He's a man of few words who has worked in the same place for the past thirty years, who watches TV, smokes, and plays the lotto. Two beers a night, a batch of spaghetti with meat sauce a week — pancakes on Sundays. He sets up a tiny TV in his room to give me as much space of my own as possible.

I kept the appointment with the shrink that the hospital made me go see. An hour and a half on public transport to visit a lazy-eyed shrink.

"My first time, I was fourteen. Tania and her brother threw a party in their basement. It was with one of Louis's friends, in his car. Lasted about a minute. He came in my hand, and I thought it smelled funny. Was just a little hand job, I don't know why it messed me up …"

"Messed, how?"

"I don't know … I was, like, obsessed with the guy. I never saw him because he went to a different school. Tania and me went to private school, but that guy, Pierre-Luc Dion, went to the big shitty high school with Louis. I couldn't stop thinking about him. I have dozens of notebooks with his name written all over them. I wrote poems about him. I would draw his cock with little hearts coming out from the tip. I was, like, crazy."

"Did you two ever see each other after the episode in the car?"

"Two years later, after prom. We were camping in this muddy field. Pierre-Luc drove up with some friends who sold speed. He saw me right away. I couldn't believe that he was there. He brought me back to his car, and I wanted to kiss him, but he shut me down. He had a girlfriend; he wouldn't cheat on her. What's worse is I knew her. And me, I remember crying a little, totally humiliated, and telling him that I could blow him better than her. He pressed play on his Eminem CD, unzipped his jeans, and … that was that."

"How did that make you feel?"

I don't want to answer his bullshit question. He insists and I look at the floor so I don't meet his googly eyes.

"At the time, I felt really great. I had won, like, when I used to swim. Yeah. That's it. Except … after that … I don't know. When I saw his girlfriend at school, all I could see was me with Pierre-Luc's limp dick in my mouth, sucking like crazy to get him hard so I could drink his cum like it was Fruitopia. I hated her, his girlfriend. She wasn't even pretty. I couldn't understand why he was dating her and not me. I was still obsessed with him two years later."

The shrink gives me homework to express my feelings about Martin "artistically," but all I can draw are ghostly figures with empty eye sockets. Instead, I tear up my childhood fairy tales that Dad was keeping to show my future children. I don't want to have kids — there are already enough of them running around.

"Terminating a pregnancy is a personal choice." It was the right decision, in the end. I would have been a fucking hostile environment.

I don't go back to see the shrink. Doesn't help worth shit. I just have to stay away from guys and I'll be okay. So I spend my days in the apartment watching the snow fall and plowing through Dad's collection of James Bond movies. Long and boring. My best friend tries to shake me out of it, but she doesn't get it.

"Saturday night. Rave in an old factory in Hochelaga. Dancing'll do you some good."

No. Not really. Martin'll be there, for sure. Or someone who knows our whole fucking story. Or worse, his new slut.

"Want to go see that China documentary … at Cinéma du Parc?"

No, thanks. I jerked him off in the back row there once, during *Laurence Anyways*.

When I call Tania on weekend mornings to invite her over for breakfast — Dad will even lend me his Tercel so I can pick her up at Longueuil metro station — she doesn't even answer. Too hungover for breakfast, I guess.

Out of sheer boredom, I cut my hair with a pair of kitchen scissors. My pixie cut is wild and almost cheerful. I'm fat now, from sitting around eating bags of chips. And since I don't wear makeup anymore, my stress zits are plain for anyone to see.

Tania was right about one thing: I need to get off my ass. Or else it won't be heartbreak that'll kill me, it'll be paralysis. I just need to pick up my swimming stuff from Mom's basement.

Fuck. Just what I need right now.

The house built into the mountainside is decorated to maximum holiday cheer. The Christmas tree is seven feet tall and half as wide, *Holy Night* plays at full blast, and Mom's tits are jacked up higher than ever. Her curly-haired little dog barks nonstop. I want to flush it down the toilet.

"Yappy's just vocal, bunny. I've never had a doggy who talked so much."

"He isn't talking, Mom, he's barking."

"Well, yes. Will you be spending the night? I've set up the guestroom."

"No. Thanks. I'm going back to Dad's."

"I don't know why you're staying there. His apartment is so small. You don't even have your own room."

"It's just for a little while, Ma."

"Here, you'd have your own living room. And a car, too. I never use mine. We could do loads of things together. It wouldn't cost you a cent."

"I'm happy at Dad's."

"I'm sure you never even see vegetables in that hole. And he smokes like a chimney. I don't know why —"

"Did you find my swimsuit?"

"Yes, and I washed it. Are you going to start training again?"

"No, I just need something to do."

"There's an Olympic swimming pool in the sports centre. Raymond has a membership. You could go with his card for free."

"I'm not going to stay with you and Ray, Mom. Thanks for the offer, but no, thanks."

"Don't get angry. I was just offering … Are you staying for supper, or are you just taking your things?"

She's made beef stroganoff in the crockpot, with egg noodles and a butternut squash soup with goat cheese crumble and, for dessert, a pecan pie. The same thing she made for Christmas supper post-Florida. She had wanted to celebrate, even though my heart was broken and her face was covered with bruises. All I wanted for Christmas that year was to never see her again. The smell of sugary pecans makes me grit my teeth.

Raymond comes back from the office and opens a beer while Mom hangs up his coat and puts his boots away.

"More soup? I swear, all your mom ever does is make soup. That and buy makeup."

"Don't you like my soup, honey?"

"We had some last weekend. Would it kill you to change it up?"

"Oh, I know. I can go to the Italian shop and pick up those frozen pizzas you like. The tomato one."

"You're crazy. You can't drive. It's snowing out. Your mom drives so bad, she's going to get into an accident, and guess who's going to have to pay to fix the car."

"You're right ... I'm not ... the best driver. I'll just go down to the cellar and get a bottle of wine."

Now I'm stuck, alone with geezer Ray, all acne scars and bug eyes. I'd bet my ass to a doughnut that he's hung like a hamster.

"So, you're staying with your dad?"

"Yeah."

"Still hasn't bought a house, has he?"

"Nope."

"Some people just aren't any good with money."

I want to knock his teeth out one punch at a time and string them around my neck.

"The world needs people like that, though. Renters, I mean. When I bought that apartment building in Saint-Jérôme, it was an investment. But those people, they're all on welfare. They live like animals. When they leave, the whole apartment needs to be stripped and rebuilt from the floor up. Nothing but trouble."

"What trouble, honey?"

"Welfare bums."

"Why, yes, you should see them, Philomena, those sad little apartments. Who lives like that, really? Raymond, would you open this bottle for me?"

"That one? Why'd you take that one?"

"I don't know … isn't it good?"

"C'mon, is your mom *trying* to be stupid? We're eating meat, Francine. How many times have I told you? Red meat — Italian wine. How many times do I have to fucking tell you?"

"I forgot, Raymond. Don't be mad."

"I'm not mad. You're embarrassing me."

Raymond goes back to the cellar to correct Mom's monumental mistake while she stares at the floor.

"He *has* told me that before …"

"Ma, why do you put up with him? He's abusing you."

"Come on, Philomena. It's just words."

My mom is stuck. Stuck and trapped in her big fucking house and her country club membership. She doesn't even *like* golf. The worst thing is that Mom is smart. She could have had a career, her own dreams, her own opinions. But no. Even a lioness can be tamed.

I go back to Dad's place, furious for her, with her. We order pizza and fries that we eat while watching *Goldfinger* and chain-smoking cigarettes.

I throw myself into doing a hundred lengths at the municipal pool every afternoon. Geezers bob in their section while I'm pushing my cardio to the limit. Old ladies wear colourful one-pieces, the old men have tattoos that have been stretched and bleached by time. Their wrinkles soothe me.

Dad's wearing the black dress shirt he puts on for big occasions: Christmas, Easter, and funerals. It's the first time I go to his factory's Christmas party.

"I'm warning you. My guys are idiots. But good idiots. They wouldn't hurt a fly."

There may be problems that champagne can't fix but fucked if I know what they are. The sparklers at the cupcake buffet glow almost as bright as I do, and I tango with one of Dad's co-workers.

My cheeks are on fire, and I stop to catch my breath next to the company's president, Michael Jorish. Smooth, well-dressed, and articulate, he turns his full attention and confidence my way. After a little small talk, the rum punch has crept up on him. He starts talking about his ninety-five-year-old mother and her terrible loneliness. His brothers live far away and can't make the time. He's in the middle of a divorce; he spends his days at the office or at his lawyers'. He doesn't have any time left over for the woman who brought him into the world and devoted her life to her children's happiness. It's breaking his heart. Not all moms are built alike.

"I should have put her in a home a long time ago, but she always refused. She says that taking her out of her home would be like yanking her heart out. She's got culture, you know, smart, too, but her memory is fading. Her body is also getting weaker. The doctors say she only has a few months left. If I don't get her into a home, she'll die alone …"

I can't help myself. "Can I help? I mean, I have a lot of spare time …"

And I need to forget. Mr. Jorish's eyes get foggy with tears, and he hugs me with so much love in his heart that I can't help but sink in. His tears smell like rum and berries as they seep into my shoulder.

I spend New Year's folding clothes and packing my few bags. Dad doesn't know what to say, just wraps his arms around me. He's proud of me. Mom left about two thousand messages on my phone, trying to get me to change my mind. "It'll scar you for life, watching that poor woman die."

She doesn't understand that I'd rather keep a dying woman company than go on a cruise with her and Ray. My mom doesn't know me at all.

5

Outremont, Winter 2013

I unpack in the empty guestroom upstairs. The hundred-year-old floors crack with my every step, the carpets are frayed, and the bookcases overflow with novels, essays, and books of poetry. All I have to do is care for Hélène Jorish when her son can't be there. A muscular male nurse comes by every day to help lift her out of bed and put her into the bath, but it's my job to scrub her down, because she's too proper to be washed by a strange man. After the bath, the nurse puts her through cursory physiotherapy and gives her IV cortisone. I spend the time when she's sleeping at the du Parc YMCA doing endless laps. On my way back, I often swing by Cheskie bakery to pick up a little treat for Hélène. She loves cream puffs and turns back into a child the moment she bites into them. After lunch, I read to her until she takes her nap.

"Would you please leave the windows open? Doesn't the sky look just like the open sea?"

While she sleeps, I can wash all the urine-soaked clothes and heat the food that the caterer dropped off. Sometimes Tania stops by for a coffee on the way to university.

"Louis can't believe that you're getting paid to babysit a grandma."

"Do you think I should invite him over?"

"Shut up, he'd freak. He'll spend hours taking pictures of every goddamn thing. My brother's become a shutter-freak."

At five on the dot, I sit Hélène down in front of the TV or a puzzle that she can only poke at. I have her eat in the parlour just outside her bedroom while listening to a classical music record, or sitting in absolute silence, depending on her mood. I have to wipe her off every two seconds — she can't stand any kind of mess. We often talk about love or art, the past getting all mixed around as we tell and retell the same stories over and again. When she finally gets tired and starts mumbling, I tuck her into bed like a little child.

"Tell me one of your stories, Phenomena."

"Okay. Uh … It was neither man nor beast. The immense Creature with webbed claws and black eyes had no heart. Instead it had a long stinging member that was always leaking a wicked venom. Vicious and insatiable, the Creature had emptied his kingdom of all women of childbearing age. His venom robbed them of their fertility, and now they roamed outside the gates of the Kingdom of Shadows. In this ashen land, happiness was nothing more than a myth. No living thing could survive or grow there."

Eyes wide with either delight or fear, I can't tell, Mrs. Jorish whispers softly that the dead always become angels in the afterlife. "Even in the Kingdom of Shadows, like my children."

"You've lost children, Hélène?"

"Yes."

"Oh, I'm so sorry. I'll tell you some other story."

"Oh, no. I love monsters. Please, go on …"

"Are you sure?"

"My husband is coming."

"Excuse me?"

"Finish telling me your love story. My husband is coming back."

"Hélène, it isn't a love story."

"Are going to tell me your story? We're going to miss our flight."

"Okay, sorry, I'll keep going. One fog-laden night, a human woman got lost and crossed the barrier into the kingdom. Weak and confused, she begged the Creature for its hospitality, only to be thrown into the castle's deepest, darkest dungeon. No one had ever seen a face as ugly as that of the Woman. The Creature, who could no longer love another being, felt a troubling emotion when the Woman, sweet and kind, cast her eyes upon his own, dark and fearsome as they were. There was no fear in the Woman's loving gaze. Shocked by this impossible wave of love, the Creature stabbed his member deep within the one he would take as his Queen of Shadows."

Mrs. Jorish is deep asleep, her hand in mine all the while.

It's a quiet, snowless morning, the first after long weeks of painful greyness. The wheelchair grinds up the paths on Mont-Royal. Hélène turns her face to the rays that peek past the bare tree branches. In this strange weather, I find myself daydreaming, as well.

"The Woman did not succumb to the venom, and as she struggled, tears fell to her feet. Small flowers sprang up in their wake."

The world heaves in terror. A thousand screaming birds leap out of the treetops, the mountain clutches me in its grasp, suddenly I can't even breathe. Martin, the crow, strolls down the black dirt path, cigarette between his lips. The sun fades to a memory. It's a nightmare. My body freezes in horror. Martin Charbonneau floats to me on the breeze. If he talks to me or tries to touch me, I'll spit in his fucking face. I hate, *fucking hate*, him. My mouth fills with bitterness; I'm dripping with venom. My body isn't readying itself to spit but to better take his cock in my mouth. I hate it.

He smiles at me casually, his eyes blank and shining. I notice how empty they are now. His heavy-lidded gaze, his black irises surrounded by yellow veiny chaos. I'm suddenly sad that he trashes his beautiful body, night after night. He greets me like a tool, and I shut my emotions off.

Hélène gets impatient. "What is going on, love?"

Nothing. Nothing is fucking happening. Her lost look finally takes Martin in, who finally lets us pass. I turn my head for a microsecond, just to confirm a suspicion. I could feel it. He's checking me out, the prick.

I climb the mountain to the lookout, digging my teeth into my lips until they bleed. Looking down on the shining city, my cell vibrates. "Wanna grab a drink?"

I shiver. I was almost cured, damn it. Almost. Why did I have to run into him? Why do all the old lovers come back to life in the springtime? It's a sign. I reply, "Nine o'clock. At Bily Kun."

I should have changed my number.

My hair is freshly washed; I put on the little black dress that he likes so much and just a touch of perfume in the hollow of my throat.

"Where are you going, love?"

"I'm going out for a drink, Hélène. Your son will be home tonight."

"My son?"

"Yes. You'll be spending the evening with Michael, lucky girl."

"Oh, my sweet Michael!"

The blanket has fallen from her thin shoulders; I lift it back up to her chin. What an amazing woman. Her skin wrinkles in delicate waves, her bright cheeks are grey and thin, and her scalp is chapped but it in no way diminishes her beauty. Her eyes are wet and red like lovely little poppies.

"Where are you going, love?"

"I'm going out for a drink …"

"I like to go dancing in the high-end clubs."

"Oh, really?"

"Yes. My mother hates it. She hates everything, such a wretch."

"I know what that's like."

"Won't you be staying?"

"No. Michael will be with you. I'll be back … later."

She starts asking the same questions all over again, asks for a story, whines, pees the bed. Michael arrives in the middle of everything, gets completely thrown by his mother acting like a child. He changes the sheets while I wash Hélène's soiled bottom with a hand towel. Fresh pyjamas, new diaper, a glass of warm milk. Michael offers to read her a story, but she screams in fear, doesn't want a stranger in her room, tries to run away, falls out of the bed, hurts herself — bad — cries like a baby. I'm the only thing that can calm her confusion tonight.

"Tell me the story, Philippine."

"All right.

"Spring had returned to the forgotten gardens. Fruit had begun to actually grow on the trees thick with sap. The sky was brightly coloured once again. Even the shadows took delight in the fresh air — it carried the promise of a marriage borne of true love. But with dawn came the shadows of vultures flying on high, ardently surveying such a fateful union. Despite this omen, the Creature and the Woman continued to savour the love they had found in such an impossible place."

Two in the morning. A sharp pain in my back brings me back to consciousness. I have fallen asleep hunched over next to Hélène, her veiny hand in mine. On my cell, a message sent at ten thirty.

"All right. I get it. Fuck you, bitch."

I don't answer. I'm going to stop picking rotten fruit.

6

Villeray, May 2016

The corpse of a five-year-old is waiting for me to do my magic and bring him back to life. He was hit by a truck while running after a balloon. Since the beginning of my career, I've mostly worked on old people. I've gotten used to their thicker skin, laugh lines, wrinkles, and crows' feet; dentures, liver spots, hairs, and warts; to their greyness, the almost complete lack of hair.

Felix Valois, my first child. Round little nose, a baby's eyelashes, broken teeth in his tiny mouth, two lips that will never discover another's body. Everything about him is so small that I have to go out and buy smaller brushes: mine are too big. Nausea grips me by the throat.

If I had kept the baby, he would be about five years old today. Would he have had that crow's beak, too?

I slide Felix back into the fridge and leave the funeral house, tears streaming all the way down to my toes.

It's getting dark already. The air is cold despite spring being underway, and I just can't go back to my empty apartment. I get Tania on the phone while she's peeing in the too-luxurious corporate bathroom of the company where she works in communications. Apparently there's money to be made in yogurt.

"I'm dying here, Tan. Want to go to Miss Villeray?"

"I'm sorry, can't. I'm in emergency meetings with the creatives for the zero percent ad. I have to convince them to hire Daniel to direct. He's got tons of talent, and it'd be sick. It'd be the best of both worlds. I'd get to work and fuck without ever leaving the ..."

All I want to do is smoke a cigarette. I hang up right away and dial Jeffrey Hudon's number.

"Well, then. She's back. How you doing, girly?"

"Bad. You still smoke?"

"Yeah. Why?"

"Are you alone?"

I step into his apartment, deep pockets under my eyes, my skin the colour of tree moss, eyes swollen from crying. He holds me against his chest, his muscles soothing me instantly.

"Happy to see you, girly."

I kiss him full in the mouth like I had seen him just the other day, though it's been months. I'm naked before I can blink. The sex is like a memory or a dream. I feel nothing, stoned by the pain. We end up spooning, his feet warm under mine.

How long did we last? Three minutes or an hour, it's all the same when you hurt that bad. He covers the back of my neck with kisses so soft that I finally break. No. Don't. Don't cry in front of him. Too late.

My tears spill over like when I was six, eight, twelve years old, and my mom was abandoning me. The first time, she left for Fort Lauderdale to live with a Jean-Paul, to "change things up a little," live the big adventure that she had always dreamed of — without me. I would stay on the South Shore with Dad. She dumped me on the steps in front of the apartment building with a suitcase and promised we would go to Walt Disney World for the holidays. I can still see her long fuchsia nails, her awful perm, and I can smell her flowery perfume. I started running after her as she walked back to the car and fell on my face. Dad picked me up. Face covered in blood and tears, I screamed at her to come back. It was too late. My heart had stopped beating. I held my Cabbage Patch Kid tight and cried myself to sleep on the sofa. Now, instead of crying I just get drunk. It's less humiliating. She abandoned me for a tan and fresh oranges, the bitch. Except her escape didn't last as long as she had hoped.

I refused to see her when she turned up at her sister's place in Chambly the next December, her face beat to shit, without a cent or her Jean-Paul. He had stayed behind with a stripper named Candy. She came to my school at lunchtime to see me, and I pretended I didn't recognize her. That Saturday, she showed up at Dad's with a new Barbie just for me. I took the present and threw it without a word into the parking lot three storeys below. Rage.

While I pick at old family scars, Jeffrey and I smoke half a pack, swaddled in a blanket. I had forgotten how bad they taste, but at least they make me stop thinking. Jeffrey's so goddamn beautiful, male and free and welcoming. He has the decency to respect my silence and doesn't treat me like a head case. I feel better already.

He fills the silence by telling me about the end of his semester, his hard work, his cramming. Caffeine and Vyvanse to stay awake, weed to fall asleep, and crushed Ritalin right before the exams. The nightmare is finally over. Clutching his diploma, he made his mom proud with typically lovely grad pictures and now hopes to get called in for an interview. In the meantime, he takes life day by day and pays rent by working at the Brasserie Laurier.

"I didn't hear from you all winter. Fucking lame, girly."

"Yeah, I know."

"I'm serious. But maybe it was a good thing. You came back with the spring."

"Ugh, lame."

We laze around, eating Kraft Dinner, snuggling as we watch nature docs, getting each other off during the end credits, followed by a second movie that we never get around to watching because he eats me out on the windowsill, and I ride him on the hallway floor. I guess they pump aphrodisiacs into the air supply around here.

* * *

Eleven thirty on Saturday morning. Felix Valois rests peaceful-ly on his white cushion. At least I hope he's peaceful. I dressed him in the clothes that his mother had brought me a few days before. She wanted him buried in his favourite shirt — a tee with a winking fox. Gritting my teeth, I slip his teddy bear in the coffin with him. My work here is done.

The funeral home is at max capacity. The smell of the bou-quets digs into my skull. I have to get out of here. A wail makes the hair on my neck stand up. His mother falls to her feet next to the coffin. People try to stand her back up, but she can only whimper. I'm helpless. I run outside, but the bright light grinds into my eyes, and I throw up on the sidewalk. Jeffrey steps out of a fire truck–red pickup and hands me a Kleenex. I wipe off the last of the oatmeal from my mouth.

"Thanks."

"Anytime, girly."

"What are you doing here?"

"Wanted to see you."

"I look like ass, Jeff."

"Your dad's fishing cabin … want to show it off for me?"

His stepdad's Dodge Ram skips along the highway, pine trees whipping by. The music crashes around our ears; the wind tosses our hair about and slaps our faces. I laugh like a little kid. Jeff lazily reaches a hand around my waist, and we share cigarette after cigarette and gobble up the landscape.

Three-and-a-half hours later, I'm back where I belong. My feet haven't even touched the ground before I start to feel the forest filling me with life. Excited to show Jeff my lake, Lake Flynn, I pull the old canoe out of the shed while he makes peanut-butter-and-magic-mushroom sandwiches.

We find ourselves alone on water buoyed by my childhood memories. We paddle like there's no tomorrow. My arms are sore, and I'm sweating like a pig, but I don't care. Happy to be with this guy that I hardly know. I see Ariel and Prince Eric reflected in the water beside us.

We stop on a rocky islet in the middle of nowhere. I'm confidently outdoorsy; I have packed masks and snorkels. We lie on a sun-warmed boulder. We put our faces in the lake. Small water spirits or minnows make our eyes go wide. We share life-changing visions. Weak light manages to break the surface surrounds Jeff's face with a ghostly halo. I'll be his first apostle.

We lie down on the moss. He tells bad jokes that crack me up for hours. I tickle him, which he hates. We squabble like children, and suddenly we're naked, and his dick is in my ass. Anal sex outdoors. That's a first.

I hear "Under the Sea" in the background.

On the way back, thunder groans over the horizon, and the wind starts to get cold. The cabin isn't far, just close enough for us to nearly get caught in the downpour. I'm convinced that swimming would be faster; Jeffrey argues with me and pisses me off, so I strip and jump into the water. The cold knocks the breath out of me, but I've felt worse. The water is molasses, gripping me hard and pulling me under. I have to swim, fast. My arms spin like windmills, my legs kick in a blur. I can't feel a thing, not the cold tearing at my body, not my heart swelling in the crushing cold. I grow weaker and weaker, but if I give up I'll look like a total pussy. No worries, just keep up my crawl and do not look at how far away the shore is. Stroke, stroke, stroke, breathe. Stroke, stroke, stroke, breathe. Seaweed slides slimily along my thighs, but I finally dig my toes into the cold silt at the water's edge. In the distance, Jeffrey is still paddling away, but he hoots my win. He looks like broccoli.

The fire crackles in the stove, and we fuck on the loveseat without taking our clothes off. Red wine, pasta in rosé sauce, cribbage tournament. We have sex on the table, naked this time, a queen of hearts stuck on his ass, plastic pegs in our hair. Later, we smoke cigarettes sitting cross-legged in jogging pants on the bed. We already have our own little traditions, and they're the best.

His warm voice throbs with bass under his three-day-old beard. "Who's your hero?"

"Frida Kahlo."

"Who's that?"

"A painter. She makes me want to be an artist."

"You paint?"

"Not as much as I'd like to. How about you? What's your passion, Jeff?"

"Doggy style."

"I already know that."

How did he end up with eyes like that? Seduction seeps out of his every pore. I ask him if he's ever cheated. Not that I care. Answer: he has.

"Regret it?"

"Yes and no. Yes, because I hurt them, and they became fucking crazy. No, because it finally ended shitty relationships."

I don't know what to say. I light up a butt to shut my slack jaw.

"I don't think I love girls the way they want to be loved. I don't believe in Prince Charming meeting his princess. I want a best friend that I can fuck. I want a real partner, not Cinderella."

"Wow. Was that Shakespeare?"

"Fuck you, girly."

"Fuck you, too."

"I'm not kidding. You're a really great girl, and I don't want to disappoint you or make you believe in fairy tales."

"Don't worry about me, Jeff. I haven't believed in fairy tales for a long time now. If I did, I still wouldn't be here with you, because you're no fucking prince. The Beast, maybe ..."

I spend all night dreaming of Frida, and we both "paint flowers so they will not die."

7

Villeray, July 2016

A heat wave is crushing the city. Daniel, Tania, Jeffrey, and I are deep into a game of Catan when the AC finally dies. All of a sudden, the piece of shit just up and quits. Pandemonium breaks out — the guys argue over how to repair it but can't get it working. Tania starts yelling, and everyone is sweating like crazy and climbing over each other with the solution. Jeffrey loses his grip, and the AC unit falls to the sidewalk, exploding in a million little pieces, nearly hitting a pedestrian, who starts screaming at us, too.

Tania is frothing. "I can't stay here, Dan. I can't breathe!"

He tells her to calm down and dials up his sketchy cousin, who sells weird odds and ends.

"No worries, peeps. My cousin Tony'll bring us an old AC. Still works, should be here in an hour or two."

Tania complains that it'll take too long. Daniel suggests going out, and she yells that's even worse. He grabs her by the arm and tells her to shut the fuck up. She spits in his face, and they fight like big idiots. The first time, I was horrified, but now it's become banal, boring. They're rolling around on the floor when Jeff tells them that we're going for a walk.

The ice cream shop has a lineup that goes around the block. Kids, dogs, old folks: everyone is begging for relief. Even covered in sweat, Jeff can turn me on. I slide the popsicle to the back of my mouth.

"A little tease, aren't you?"

We run to the neighbourhood pool, struggling to stay conscious, beat a path through the bikinis and banana-hammocks and lock ourselves in the handicapped stall. We fuck standing up, hands pressed against the graffiti on the painted cement. His jizz slides down my thigh. I'm nowhere near coming. We walk back to the apartment in slow motion, not even holding hands, it's so goddamn hot.

"My cousin installed the AC. For free. Look what I bought off him as a thank you."

Four beans of MDMA in a little baggie slip out of his pocket. Tania, super excited, squeals that we should try. I don't know, I have work tomorrow … Jeffrey swallows his pill with a glass of wine, no fucking around. Shit. Chemicals have always scared me. Daniel swears it's good; his cousin only sells dope shit.

* * *

I'm becoming a diamond, the one from the Pink Floyd song. Tingle, tingle in the tips of my funny fingers. Fingers. Cocktail weenies with wings. Cock, tail, weenies. I deep throat a Molotov cocktail, smile spreading into a squint. Taniel and Dania make love delicately on a leather couch that eats up pieces of bread, small change, a TV remote, my hot, hot, hot, heart, a big thick wool blanket on my shoulders, a walking dead ghost haunting the frozen conditioned air. A guitar lick makes my legs go numb and my pussy throb.

Jeffrey, Jeffrey, come over here, you menace, dance, dance, take me in your loving arms, tell me that diamonds are forever, tickle me down to my toes with your voice that makes me catch fire. My friends laugh, blending in with the wall like plaster statues. Daniel is nice and really smart, and they're a cute couple. So alive, and I love them. Rough sex from time to time, that's fine — there's nothing wrong with that. Christian Children's Fund ads we can all remember; we can't forget those little African kids with swollen bellies. A memory, like the Barbie I called Assface, and my third-grade teacher who killed herself over Christmas break. Some tampons hurt my cervix, we have too much stuff, consumer culture is killing us.

Every cigarette shared with Jeffrey Hudon makes me feel alive. Smoking indoors makes me feel super alive. Wham bam, so alive.

"I had quit smoking, Jeff. I had quit to encourage my dad. You know he has to drag an oxygen tank around with him? It's okay, though. His cancer'll go away; it's just an itty bitty little cancer. Me, I'm not going to smoke all my life. I'll quit soon, for sure. I'm telling you, I gotta tell you, I'll quit soon. I love my dad. He's trying so fucking hard. Dad's the best. He's so strong, been through so much. Did you know my parents got divorced when I was six?"

"No, I didn't know. I'm glad you're telling me, Philly. Come on, come on over here."

"I was sad because, because it would have been nice if they had been in love, together their whole lives, but in the end, it's okay, because my dad is the toughest. I know he'll get better."

"For sure, babe ..."

"Babe?"

"Babe. It's good, babe, it's you, Philly."

"Babe is a pink little piggy."

"I really want to kiss you."

"So many piggies are dying, Jeff."

"Kiss me, babe."

Soft, safe warm lips. His tongue dances on mine like the water beetles on Lake Flynn. Standing up, sitting down, on a windowsill, standing, sitting, cute little cuties, little menace, standing up, two steps forward, one step back, lighter, fire, fire, pretty fire, smoke, walk, sit, smoke, tongue, tongue, stick your tongue down my throat, down to my heart, you're so goddamn beautiful, Jeffrey Hudon.

"No, you're beautiful, Philomena. I love your name, your tits, your tie-dye hair ... I ever tell you you're the most beautiful woman I ever met? You're so hot with your long hair — you're making me hard."

"Did I ever tell you about Hélène Jorish?"

"No. You're so beautiful when you talk. Talk more, talk to me, please, talk to me."

"Okay, we'll light ourselves a cigarette with the lovely lighter, and I'll talk to you some more. Mrs. Jorish was an old lady I looked after for the last few months of her life. I was with her at the end."

"That's fucking beautiful."

"Dead people fart. Did you know that? Always makes me laugh."

"Were you scared?"

"Of farts?"

"Of her dying."

No, death isn't scary. Die, die, die in my arms tonight, hurt me softly, whip me with your tongue, pull my angel hair, cuff my wrists to yours. I want to call you Master. Take me, babe, take me before I dissolve into the rest of humanity. Fuck my body, my soul, you're so goddamn beautiful. A jaw cut with a goddamn chisel. When I was twenty years old, we cooked little bits of hash on a knife in a busted toaster oven. I burned my face a lot. Your face falls apart, my love, your nose is gone, your hands are huge, your mouth is a sewer drain, you're a Picasso. I'M IN LOVE WITH YOU, JEFF HUDON.

8

The shy morning sun is covered with thunder-thick black clouds. Tania and Daniel are smoking a dessert spliff, Louis is snoring like a Mack truck, and Raphael is cheerily washing dishes. On the porch, I wish I could rip my rib cage open with my fingernails. Frothy white water dashes itself on the shore, seagulls' screams break the hushed throbbing, stun the beating of my heart, on its last legs. I don't have the strength to hold back the monster eating my insides anymore. It keeps crooning "Shine On You Crazy Diamond" at me ...

I want to run away in my old Tercel, drive through the storm all the way back to Quebec. Hell, not even stop, catch a plane to Vancouver, no bags, just adrenalin.

Even if the West Coast is three hours behind, I would never arrive in time. She's already taken your name by now.

Fuck B.C.

I start running nowhere fast. The barbed leaves on the endless cornstalks tear my skin. A cramp pierces my side. I run, run, run into the growing darkness, never looking back, throw myself into the dense woods. Trees on my right; more trees on my left. I run along the path. The waves whisper for me to follow.

I clamber up a massive hill on all fours like a bitch. The Gaspé sea fills the edges of my horizon. I feel its rage: I want to throw my bones onto the cliffs, too.

I can see the Córdoba sun shining on me, like when I was eighteen. I jumped that time, freed myself of fear, jumped out of the plane with wings sprouting from my back. Could the fall still be as thrilling ten long years later? Just this morning I was sitting next to Raphael like a stranger, chewing tasteless food and pretending to laugh, smiling at the right times so that no one could see how badly I want to die.

But Tania knows. She can feel it.

Raphael made a toast. "I want to wish you a happy birthday, Philly. I hope you have a year that's as amazing as you are and hope you know how honoured I am to be part of your life. Never, not in my wildest dreams, would I have ever thought that you would one day let me love you so completely and start a family with you. Here's to you turning twenty-nine, and our beautiful baby inside you — I just hope it has your eyes! Happy birthday, my love!"

9

Villeray, August 2016

Another sticky afternoon. I show up to the funeral home completely fucked. Way too many dead people for my summer of endless parties. Tania and me, we spend our nights singing karaoke and drinking vodka-pickle shots in Jeff's brewery. Daniel meets up with us after his late-night editing, and we drink wine and smoke weed and solve all the world's problems until well after the sun comes up. And, since the beginning of the summer, Jeff and I don't sleep, we just fuck.

Fully collapsed on my bed, I get a text. "Get dressed, babe. I'm at Huis Clos." I'll never sleep again.

I run like a madwoman in new high-heeled sandals that go perfectly with the cute vintage dress that clings to my hips.

Sitting at our table, our favourite because of its position — close to the toilets for a key bump or a quickie, or both — Jeffrey is waiting for me with an open bottle of champagne. He's wearing that amazing white linen shirt, casually unbuttoned. My sexy beast. Our glasses clink and he licks the drop of Moët that has rolled down my lower lip.

"You're such an *animal* …"

Our waiter, Hugo, drops off a plate of oysters on the table. Its liquid flesh slides down my throat while Jeff's hand teases my pussy. I know better than to wear panties by now. Can anyone tell that I'm getting fingered in the middle of the room? Are they jealous? I hope so. If not, pretending to like it is all for nothing. I let out a satisfied sigh to stroke his ego and get him to stop. Feeling like a king after getting his girlfriend off in three flicks, Jeff swallows a bounty of bubbles.

"What is all this for?"

"Because you're an amazing woman, and you deserve the best."

"That's *so sweet*. But, really?"

"I have an interview with a tech startup. A finance consultant position has opened up, my stepdad knows the VP, so …"

"Shit! Congrats!"

I jump on him and cover his face with lipstick.

We don't care; it's amazing, and I'm so proud. He slows me down. It's just an interview, exciting, but not a lock, yet. I know, but I believe in him. The job's as good as his. He can't help but smile, seeing the future he's always wanted slowly coming into being in front of his eyes.

The moon is just a thin scratch brightening the fall of night. Sitting on the hood of his pickup, we look down on the city from the top of the mountain. The August wind rises; I burrow into Jeff's big strong arms that I love so much. We're so fucking beautiful. I can tell just how jealous we make every other couple feel. We finally look the way we've always felt.

"I have to tell you something about the job."

"What?"

"If I get it, I'll have to move to Toronto."

"How long."

"I'll have to live there, Philly. That's where the job is."

My dreams crash to pieces.

I restart Mrs. Germanotta's manicure for the third time. I can't concentrate today, and it shows in my work. If only I could blame her, like, "Stop fidgeting, goddamn it." But I can't. She's dead. The solemn silence around me makes me want to explode.

I light up a cigarette on rue Jean-Talon. Bought myself a pack, like an idiot. At least I'm independent in my self-destruction. I don't need Jeffrey Hudon, for sure. A missed call and a text from him inviting me to have lunch. Fuck that. The last puff sticks in my throat.

Ten long red nails bring back the days when she was young and wild. I based her makeup on the pictures her husband handed me with shaking hands. She looks amazing in the cliché wedding pictures, an Italian beauty with an actress's nails and love in her eyes. The old lady in front of me has the face of someone who loved and laughed heartily and ate lots of pasta. Even dead, she looks more alive than me. I really nailed the blush, though … Am I going to die old and dignified and loved, too? No. The way things are going, I'm going to die alone, because my allergies mean I can't even get a cat.

I'm sorry, Mrs. Jorish. I got the story wrong. I'll just restart, okay? You'll rest better this way.

"It was neither man nor beast. The immense Creature with rippling muscles and teal eyes had no heart but a microscopic little needle from which his fluids dripped pathetically."

I knew he'd get it. I knew he'd get it, that he'd charm the interviewers with his pretty-boy face and his languid confidence. He's going to Toronto, the douche. I've been pulling back for the past few days, so he would start to miss me, so he realizes I'm more important than Toronto. It's working. He's still reaching out to me. I stubbornly start working on Mrs. Germanotta's hair. She would curl her hair, so I work the heating iron until her face is perfectly framed. I'm so fucking ugly. My hair is greasy, and I need to shave. What do I care if I turn into a cave-woman? He's moving to Toronto, fucking idiot. I'm not going to sleep sprawled across his big naked chest anymore. No more banging in restaurants, no more all-nighters and double dates.

* * *

The warm water flows like the Iguaçu Falls down my skull. I miss Argentina, miss being wild. It was so amazing. Tania and I were slack-jawed when we saw Devil's Throat, two little women in the making staring down a force of nature. We were so great. No makeup, au naturel, hairy as fuck. These days I shave for a guy who has basically broken up with me.

A knock at the door. It's not like I can ignore it, even though I look hypoglycemic, and the bags under my eyes go all the way down to my knees. Jeff is there, pizza and a six-pack in hand.

"Happy birthday, babe."

We eat like pigs in awkward silence, then we chain-smoke cigarettes in patio chairs.

"Can we talk?"

"I don't know, Jeff. I really don't know what you want to talk about."

"Okay, for starters, why haven't I heard from you in a week? You ignore me and don't want to see me. What's going on?"

"I don't owe you anything."

"True, but you don't have to ignore me like a little kid. That's not us, babe."

"Really? What is *us*, then? Fucking off to the other side of the country just like that? That us, babe?"

My negativity pisses him off. Too bad. I'm not going to lose this fight. I want to chuck him off the balcony and punch him all the way down. He clears his throat, getting ready to cave. Take that, loser.

"Philly, we have two options: either we break up or you come to Toronto with me."

I'm dumbstruck, stupefied, as if he had started singing in Chinese. Tears tickle my eyes, fucking shit. I bite my lip. I can't give in — show emotion — but my stomach churns so bad it hurts. I'm starting to cramp up. Fucking greasy pizza and fucking cigarettes punching my insides out. One big drop of cold sweat slides slowly down my spine. Jeff grows more and more uncomfortable as the silence stretches on.

"Can you at least say something? Anything?"

"I need to shit."

I'm bent double with stomach pain in the bathroom. The last time I had diarrhea this bad I was eight, and my mom had just been granted full custody. She made me live with her, her boyfriend, Marc, and his two pimply teenagers in a huge house in Boucherville. I had never seen my dad so pissed. He punched a hole in the wall so deep I got scared that monsters would start to pour out. My look of fear immediately stopped his rage dead. He picked me up in a hug, promising to keep taking me to movies at the Cineplex. I'd still have a room at his place, and we could even repaint it in the summertime. After a thousand hugs and a million kisses, Mom dragged me out of the apartment and buckled the seatbelt around my aching belly. While she was trying to figure out just how badly I needed to go, Marc kept telling her to stop giving in to me all the time and to get in the car so we could finally leave. She caved. My mom, the good obedient pet. I was writhing with pain, farting mustard gas, whining that I had to go so bad, but fat Marc didn't want to pull over so I could relieve my irritable bowels. "You're a big girl, Philomena. You can hold it for five minutes." So, I flooded the back seat of his brand spanking new car with uncontrollable diarrhea — and my conscience stayed perfectly clean. It was all over my jeans and shoes, staining the seat, up the backrests, and down to the floor mats. Even after two weeks of deep cleaning, his Volvo still smelled like shit. My stomach hurt for two-and-a-half years, until they finally broke up.

"Congrats on the job. I knew you'd get it." The sun is setting behind the Notre-Dame-du-Rosaire's belltower. Kids are playing ball in the alley while their parents yell at them to come to supper. "I didn't know you'd consider living with me. That was a surprise."

"With you, I'd be up for it"

"And my dad? If he needs me?"

"Toronto is only seventy-five minutes from Montreal. Hardly even a flight."

"And my job?"

"Every city has funeral homes, Philly."

"Okay. What about Tania, our apartment? I can't just leave — we just planted flowers on the balcony …"

"You think too much, babe."

"No. I don't. I'm being responsible. I mean … I want to go with you, but …"

"But what?"

"What'll I do in Toronto?"

He hands me his cell, browser open on a page for an art school in an up-and-coming part of town. I'm fucked. I want to. I'm going to say yes.

Jeffrey takes my face in his hands, tells me that he's got a good feeling about this. He tells me how we'll leave our place in the mornings, him to work, me to school, eat in trendy restaurants, fuck absolutely everywhere in and out of the apartment, talking English, meeting new people, get a dog — why not?

Nothing can stop us. We can do anything.

10

Toronto, October 2016

Nude models change everything. It's good for my soul to draw a live, breathing human being, a body that breathes, shivers, and sometimes breaks into hysterical nervous laughter. Seeing a whole body without being able to touch it drives me absolutely crazy. In a good way. Only I can't share this energy with Jeff. He's always at work. He stays at the office super late, comes back home at insane hours, starts his shifts in the middle of the night, comes home cranky and exhausted. We haven't fucked in weeks. I decorated our tiny apartment on my own. I explore the city and try out new restaurants — on my own. Jeff doesn't even seem to like his job, he's just being eaten alive. Then, a miracle: a whole weekend, just the two of us. The first since we arrived. We'll go hiking, then spend a day at a spa being pampered and loving each other to death. I need to feel his skin against mine again.

He steps into the apartment and crumples onto the sofa, bleary eyes digging deep into his skull from lack of sleep. I straddle him, trying to ease his tension with endless kisses, asking questions about his day.

"Fine," he says.

Okay. Good. I'll do all the talking, then. I give him every detail about the Mexican visual artist who so impressed me and my new classmate, Liam Albanese.

"They teach you how to shut the fuck up yet?"

The slap comes out of nowhere, so hard that it leaves fingerprints embossed into his face. Stunned by my reaction, he pushes me off of him, goes to pull out a bottle of whisky. He pours a glass, throws it back, pours another, and goes out onto the balcony to smoke. Like two hyenas sharing a cage.

I microwave some frozen food, trembling from head to toe the whole time. I can't eat a bite. I'll just throw it back up. Jeff chain-smokes outside despite the autumn rain. We look straight out of a soap opera.

When he finally opens the patio, eyes red from crying, we hug each other hard, each unable to break the silence between us. He ends up falling asleep in my arms, warm in our bed. I stare at the ceiling all night.

I jolt awake in the brutal morning light, blinded by the naked white walls. He's just getting back from a walk-in clinic with a Vyvanse prescription, just like college days.

"I don't know why I didn't think of it before, babe! I'm so dumb. This'll change everything, make it like it was before. I'll start going back to the gym, get fitter, happier. I'll be able to work better again. Everything'll be fine."

"What about us?"

"*What* about us?"

"When's the last time we had sex?"

"Don't start, Philly."

"No. I'm serious. When was the last time? Because I can't remember."

"Stop being such a drama queen."

"We don't do anything together anymore! We don't laugh, we don't fuck, you don't sleep …"

"The pills will change all that! Everything'll go back to how it used to be."

"For real? Pills'll change all that?"

"Yes. I promise."

He swallows the orange and blue caplet with a swig of coffee. He kisses me, but it's cold, impersonal. Like he doesn't care. He takes my clothes off and goes down on me mechanically. We fuck awkwardly until he comes on my stomach. He yanks the old gym bag out from under the bed and heads off to work out. He'll be back in two hours, he says. He kisses me on the forehead and leaves me hanging like a fucking idiot.

So much for the spa and the hike. Weather's shit, anyway.

11

Toronto, December 2016

The city is a polar vortex. Jeff is doing so well at work that he's been given a bonus and a bunch of major clients. More demanding clients. When Dad asked if we'd be coming to Montreal for Christmas, I could hear something wrong in his gasping voice.

"Don't worry, Philly. It's just that … the cancer is just … smarter than we thought. I'll have to do … some chemo."

I promise that Jeff and I won't let him go through it alone.

"How you doing, Philly? How's Toronto?"

I lie because the truth is too ugly to say out loud. Jeff won't get it up for me, we only argue, he's fuelled on amphetamines and whisky on the rocks. And I'm turning into a crazy bitch. Yep, I logged on to his computer and found his massive porn history. Nope, there was no thoughtful jewellery or intimate dinner or "I love you" for our six-month anniversary. He did, though, throw an eighth of weed on the kitchen counter, hoping that'd calm me down. I've spent the past two weeks getting high as fuck, drawing monsters alone in our living room. Couple of the year, us.

"It was neither man nor beast. The heartless Creature with rippling muscles and glowing green eyes was enormous."

Heartless, no fucking shit.

"Nevertheless, the Woman and the Creature were ever as one; nothing could tear them apart.

"And yet the vultures that still circled overhead cast shadows upon the Creature's mind. This love was false, laughable, unworthy of his eternal majesty. The Woman would inevitably seek to usurp his throne. Horrified at the idea of losing his kingdom, the Creature coiled his member around her throat and snuffed her out. The new-found silence was serene. Such was the price of peace, of true contentment. The sound of her breathing would no longer trouble the still air …"

The drawing workshop is decorated with cardboard snowflakes and bright colourful garlands, and a buffet's been set out to mark the end of classes. Liam is a total sweetheart — going on and on about last night's Tinder date with an uncontrollable smile turning up the corners of his mouth. The beginning of a relationship is always so exciting … I have to explain to him that, sorry, Jeff is too important to spend a Friday night eating egg salad sandwiches with us. I hit the free wine a little too hard, laugh a little too loud at every joke, and eat like a fucking hog. Five shots of tequila and two line dances later, I say good-bye to Liam Albanese and, unwittingly, to Toronto.

The buildings are covered with Christmas decorations, and carols echo in the largely empty streets. The green-glass sky-scrapers look like giant diamond pillars. At the end of Green Avenue, the Irish Pub twinkles in the night. That's where he likes to bring potential clients. What about me? Fuck it — I'm taking Philly out tonight.

As expected, he's at a big table surrounded by business-men. He's laughing like a fucking brown-noser. You want to laugh, babe? Then watch this shit. I jump on him, knocking over pints of beer, and kiss him full on the mouth while rub-bing my tits all over his wet shirt. Jeff hates losing control. He laughs uncomfortably and tries to get me to shut up, but I scream that I want to suck him off, loud enough for the whole bar to hear. Maybe that was a little too much. Oops.

He grabs me by the arm and drags me outside. I laugh and cry at the same time, nose leaking, mouth filling with thick white spit.

I want to hit him, hurt him, hold him tight against me. I yell that he's ruining my life, that he's shit in bed, that the only thing we have in common anymore is the fucking cigarettes that we smoke. "Moving here was the worst idea we ever had."

He stops me still and forces me to meet his eyes.

"No, we don't have anything in common anymore. Yes, our sex life is shit. Moving here is the best decision I've made in my entire life. Just not with you."

He shoves me into a cab and walks away without looking back.

It's been three days and nights that I've been living in numbing pain on my dad's beige futon. I'm using my suitcases as bed-side tables. The only good thing is that I've stopped smoking. I'm too tired to get up, to find the pack, to take the cigarette out, to light it, or to even breathe. I don't want to do anything anymore. Tania and Daniel, who've been living together since I suddenly left town, offered that I come live with them, but I couldn't stand the thought of sleeping in Jeff's old room. He hasn't spoken to me since the tense morning when I woke up, disgustingly hungover, to find my bags packed at the door. When I said we should talk about it, he took another fucking pill and ran away to the gym. He'd left a one-way ticket to Montreal on the counter.

My dad rushes out of his room and throws up in the toilet. His chemo is as violent and painful as love. I bury myself under the quilt until I can't breathe anymore.

I don't go outdoors even once over the holidays. He didn't write me a single time. When the clock struck twelve on New Year's, my only wish was that my head would explode into a cloud of confetti.

12

Longueuil, late February 2017

Tania dragged my ass off the futon. I whined that I couldn't leave the apartment if my life depended on it, that I had to stay close for my dad — I even used the word *cancer* to show how much I meant it — but it had no effect because Tania is a Russian spy at heart.

"I have to get him groceries …"

"On a Friday night?"

"Uh-huh."

"You're full of shit, Philly. You just went — the fridge is full of Ensure. Also, your dad told me that you drink half of what you buy him. That's fucking gross. Even I wouldn't do that. You can't eat solid food?"

She knows how to wake me up.

Daniel and Tania bought themselves a car — a big step for any couple. He wanted an SUV; she wanted a convertible. They fought and finally bought a used BMW. It's great. They're so lucky. I'm happy for them. The smell of bubble gum air freshener is so cheery, I want to punch it in the face.

Dressed in black from head to toe, I look like I'm going to my own funeral.

"Don't make a face, Philly. You're going to have fun tonight. And it's important for the guys that you show up."

Last summer Daniel directed his first short film with some government money. After a few days of shooting, and months of audio and video editing, mixing, and a few existential crises, the movie is finally finished. The story is touching and real, and Louis, Tania's brother, my almost-brother, was director of photography, which makes the film look a whole lot better than its budget. I'm proud of them. My face just can't move to express it properly.

The second we get to the Rialto theatre, I rush to the bar for a double whisky on the rocks. It tastes like him. I just want to bury my head under a mountain of pillows.

The lights finally dim, and a tall redhead finally makes his way onto the stage to stand in the spotlight. He's wearing square black glasses and a sober suit — with a wooden bow tie to keep things whimsical — and gives the crowd an enormous smile. "Ladies and gentlemen, dear guests, welcome to the second edition of the Nitrate Film Festival, celebrating excellence in short film."

Cue thunderous applause. While the way-too-energetic MC explains in perfect diction how the evening will proceed, my head swivels like crazy, looking for a waiter. If I get drunk enough, I just might make it through. Mr. Woody Bow Tie makes painfully bad jokes to the rest of the room. Which is worse: the jokes or the audience that actually laughs at them? Where is the fucking waiter?

Chaos, Daniel's film, opens the festival. The scenes are breathtaking: the landscape of his long-lost homeland, an actress with translucent skin, a blond kid with a zit-covered face, two naked bodies making sweet, slow love to each other on a rat-bitten mattress. I miss having his goddamned arms around me. The whole theatre laughs when two drunk teens play Punch 4 Punch on an empty North Shore street in the middle of the night. Awkward silence stills the air when a young girl pulls out a forgotten tampon, and a wave of tears hits everyone when the young man throws himself off an overpass. Hard to believe that ten minutes of illusion can make you feel so much. The final scene takes place in a dim bar. A slow panning shot around a young girl dancing her heart out on the floor. What the fuck? There. In the back of the room, behind the girl, he's right there. Pretending to pour beer for the clients, his linen dress shirt and sexy fucking face. Jeffrey Hudon, forever immortalized in *Chaos*. Cut to black, roll credits, applause.

I punch the toilet stall in the unisex bathroom, bite my forearms until they bleed. A single tear sneaks from my eyes and down my nose almost without my noticing. Tania climbs onto the neighbouring stall's toilet, looking for me. "Philly? Philly, look at me. I know it hurts, I know you think you'll never be happy again, but trust me — you'll get better. Get up, you're sitting in a puddle of piss."

She hugs me tight like she always does, pushes my hair back, and feeds me her unconditional love.

"I'm taking you straight home the second the projector stops."

The lights come back on in the Rialto, and the PR work can finally begin. I congratulate Daniel in a mumbling voice. He holds me tight and gives me a kiss on the forehead. Louis sneaks up on us from behind. Now I'm caught in a group hug with two overjoyed peacocks, and I feel the colour coming back to my cheeks. The MC joins our group, shakes hands, and congratulates Daniel and his team. His gaze finally falls on me. Please, please don't talk to me ...

"Hi. I'm Raphael, one of the festival organizers."

"Yeah, hi."

"Did you also work on the film?"

"No. I'm just a friend."

Raphael hands me a glass of bubbly. No fucking way am I staying. I force a smile and bolt away to hide in the crowd, someplace safe. I see Jeffrey in the champagne, remember the oysters, sunrise morning sex, the Deli Plus that changed my life. Oh my god, Jeff. Where are you, Jeff? What are you doing? What happened to us? Do you miss me at all? JEFF!

Tania has started dancing, glued to Daniel; their tongues do a tango all across the room. I don't want to ruin their party, so I sneak away and wind up on du Parc.

The air is cold and wet, the snowbanks are half gravel, and all the cars are dirty; everything looks ugly and rundown and heartbreakingly sad. I walk the streets without looking at where I'm going and wind up in front of Cheskie bakery, two blocks from the YMCA. There are no coincidences. The bell dings as I walk in, just like I remember it. The enormous baker who has worked there since forever hands me my millionth-and-one cream puff.

Standing in front of the Victorian house on Bloomfield, I stare at the window on the south wall, Mrs. Jorish's bedroom window. My chin is covered in whipped cream, my tears mix with the snot running down my nose, and I cry in hiccups like a little kid.

13

Chicoutimi, March 2017

The spring sun shines off the peaks in the Laurentides wildlife reserve. Tania is doing her eyelids while Louis and I, in the back seat, share a joint while discussing the finer points of *New Phone* by Loud, advance copy courtesy of Daniel Torrès, who knows absolutely everyone who's important.

Daniel steers the BMW with a loose hand, buzzing that *Chaos* is an official selection of the Look Film Festival, a dream he's had forever. I came along because I was promised a party, a distraction. Just have to keep my eyes shut for the last thirty seconds of the film. Or not.

We rented a house in the middle of Chicoutimi for the occasion, a typical bungalow built in the sixties with era decor. I snag the little bedroom with a knitted still life on the wall. The dutiful child of divorce, I unpack all my clothes and survey my new digs.

We dress up and drink cocktails in the living room. Daniel takes forever to choose the record he wants to play — he's brought a whole suitcase full of them. Ridiculous. Tania's getting impatient. Louis takes pictures of everything with a vintage film camera, pissing her off even more. She jumps at him, nearly skewering my hand with her high heel. Feels just like being back in the old Reynier living room, circa 1992, or 2007. It was always the same thing when I went over to Tania's place: they would fight because Louis would goof around, and I would end up trampled by the two elephants in the room. Sometimes, their fighting would just go on and on, so I'd go chat with their parents until the storm passed. That is, if the adults weren't fighting, too. When that was the case, I'd just cross the yard and come back the next day.

Finally, Nina Simone pulses through the walls, and all the tension drains out of us. Daniel dims the lights, ice cubes clink in our glasses, and we drain the bottle of Ungava. And a bottle of white wine. And another of red. I roll around the puce shag carpet. Daniel is tired from the drive up and falls asleep on the sofa. Tania curls up with him. Louis wants to get going, so I throw my fur coat on, and we walk up rue Racine arm in arm, like a couple of newlyweds.

"Why haven't we ever made out, Louis?"

"Because I'm not a fan of incest, I guess."

The downtown is deserted, with nothing but the Chicoutimi Hotel shining in the night. The lobby is packed with young filmmakers, the music buzzes in the stereos, and cast and crew alike look us up and down like fresh meat. We hardly have enough time to down our first shot when a mob with starry eyes ensnares Louis.

"Did your tattoo, like, hurt a lot? What was it like to shoot a movie with Daniel Torrès? You're his girlfriend's brother, right? Are you really going to do Alaclair Ensemble's next video?"

The five blonds swallow him up, and he disappears from sight. Meh.

I catch a girl looking at me in the mirror and stop, stunned. I look completely different, dressed like a femme fatale and with makeup on. Different with my heart broken, I guess. A guy leers at me without any shame at all. An actor in a casually unbuttoned shirt, with sexy eyes and a practised smile. I've seen him before onstage and in short sketches at Jeffrey's brewery.

"Mind if I sit next to you?"

What's nice about actors is that you can toy with them without even feeling bad. I shrug and take a mouthful of my drink. His name is Sebastien Strasbourg, twenty-six, like me. Single, like me.

"I heard you're a bad guy."

"Who told you that?"

"All the girls you've slept with."

"Maybe they're the ones who're bad."

"Maybe."

His checkered shirt seems very soft, so I let my hand drift across the pattern down to his designer ripped jeans until I make his cock hard. He chugs the rest of his beer, I pound my whisky, and he almost carries me to the third floor, to his room at the end of the hall.

The door barely has enough time to close before I'm on all fours sloppily sucking him off. The room smells like mothballs, like the cabin at Flynn Lake. I tease the tip. My knees are starting to get rug burned. I really could squat in these heels, but don't want to lose my balance. Three months I've been thinking about Jeff's cock. Three months I've been keeping myself from sucking any nameless guy off just to fill the void. Fuck it. Tonight I'm Sharon Fucking Stone. Sebastien Strasbourg roars like a bull when he comes down my throat.

"Can I have something to drink, please?"

"Uh, yeah … uh, sure … sorry. It's been a long time … Is a pop okay?"

"What do you mean?"

"Uh … I usually don't come so fast. You just … took me by surprise. I'm really sorry."

"It's okay."

After a big chug and a huge echoing burp, I redo my lipstick to look classy again and get back to the party.

"Uh … Well, yeah. Uh, thanks? For the head?"

"No prob. Thanks for the Sprite."

We wait for the elevator in awkward silence. When the doors finally open, coked-up idiots flood out, yelling like morons, beer spilling all over the hallway. A girl tries to open a locked door like a mental patient.

"Yo, Cat. You're so fucking dumb. This isn't even the right floor."

They burst out laughing and kick open the door to the fire escape. Strasbourg and I take refuge in the elevator. Just before the doors close, I see the door to room 312 open. An old lady with see-through skin stares at me, teary eyed and trembling. She looks strangely familiar.

"Are you the one who woke me up? You're a terrible young woman."

"Huh? No. No, ma'am. I wasn't the one who tried to open your door."

Dad. Her eyes are hollowed out like my dad's. What the fuck am I doing here? Why am I always in the wrong place? Terrible, Philly, terrible young woman.

"Please, let me sleep. I'm very sick."

Yeah. Me, too.

I wake up with a lurch. Tania and Daniel's headboard is knocking against the bedroom wall like crazy. Who fucks at eight o'clock in the fucking morning? I roll to my feet to throw up in the bathroom. The floor tiles are fucking freezing. I can see chimney smoke rising lazily through the sheer curtains. Seven months and twelve days ago, Jeffrey and I went down to the train tracks and took a microdose of LSD. We lay down on the yellow grass to watch smoke from the factories join with the clouds overhead. My head was resting on his chest, and he ran his fingers through my hair. He always loved my long blond hair.

Louis, back from a morning jog, suggests that we eat a quick breakfast, then go see the highlight program in the university auditorium. The man is a machine. Tania moans louder than ever. For lack of better options, we get moving.

A kindly volunteer welcomes us with a wide smile. I hate that everyone else is so happy. Slouching back into my seat, cozily draped in my dad's XL factory sweater, I close my eyes and start to faze everything out. But I feel something, someone, on my left. It's Bow-Tie-Raphael, cheery despite the ungodly hour.

"Hey, Philomena. It's great to see you in my part of town."

"Hi."

"Enjoying your stay in Saguenay?"

"Uh-huh."

"Tomorrow, we're going skating with the guys from Nitrate, if you want to come. A little exercise does wonders for a hangover!"

"What do you mean?"

"Uh ... I mean ... just kidding ..."

I throw the hoodie over my head and fall asleep after the second short.

The bungalow is packed with beautiful people, the fireplace is lit, a Wu-Tang vinyl is spinning, there's coke on every horizontal surface and buds of Sour Diesel in all the candy dishes. Daniel's party is a lavish celebration. The jury's first prize in his category, twenty thousand dollars to jump-start his next project. Louis sabres open a bottle of champagne; screams of joy and general scramble to get a taste of his victory. I look mysterious in my long dress. It's so tight that I have a hard time breathing. I laugh slowly, hidden behind sunglasses like a movie actress. I kiss the rim of my glass until it's covered in red.

More and more people fill the house as the night and the party move on. I'm so stoned I can't feel my teeth or my legs, and I yell every word. Louis and I do a spontaneous samba across the floor. We move too quickly, faces blur, and I stumble dizzily and fall into Sebastien's waiting arms. I kiss him with tongue and unzip his pants while he whispers into my ear that tonight will be my birthday party.

"My birthday's at the end of summer, when all the leaves die. Not in the middle of the winter, you fucking idiot."

He must like the abuse, because he starts leading me down to the basement. I stagger along the walls and knock into Christmas decorations. Somehow Sebastien has slipped his head up my dress and is eating me out with his juicy lips. Fake snow sticks to my ass while tears stream down my face.

"The sound of her breathing would no longer trouble the still air … But, before her last sigh, the Woman caressed the

Creature with her hand. The Creature's grip loosened and, for the first time in its life, it began to gently weep. For a moment, they were both truly alive."

I interrupt Sebastien's hard work. Obviously, I won't be able to get off tonight.

Finally alone, I throw myself at a rotary phone and dial his number.

"Jeffrey à l'appareil."

"Hi!"

"Hello?"

"It's me."

His silence goes up like a wall. Why doesn't he say anything? Maybe the line is faulty. Or maybe he's too emotional to speak.

"Jeff, it's me."

"Philly?"

"Yes! Yeah, it's me."

"Oh."

"I fucking miss the sound of your voice, babe."

"Philly, I can't talk right now."

"Wait! I need to ask you a question."

"Can we talk later?"

"Why did we break up, eh? Really. What's the real reason? We should never have broken —"

"Are you drunk?"

"You and me, we love each other so much. More than anyone else! Remember us? Remember the cottage?"

"I met someone, Philomena."

Motherfucker. Time slows down, tearing me apart. Time is killing me.

"That's okay. That's fine. She's just a rebound."

"No. It's ... serious, Philly. I quit my job, and we're starting up a food truck in Jasper."

"The *what*?!"

"I'm sorry about Toronto. I was depressed ..."

"Wait. You love her?"

" ... yes."

"I don't fucking believe you!"

"Look. It was love at first sight. Angelica —"

"Angelica? What the fuck kind of name is that?"

"Call me when you're sober, okay?"

"You're a fucking asshole, Jeff Hudon!"

"Okay. Bye, Philly."

"Can your fucking whore even fuck you like me, Jeff? Or can you *still* not get it up? I'm fucking every fucking —"

He's hung up. I'm alone on the line, with spit running down the receiver.

I cross the kitchen, ignoring all the looks people are giving me, pick up a bottle of vodka, and open the door to the snowy yard. I drink like a baby sucking a teat and collapse into a pile of snow, body numbed to heat, cold, alcohol, pain, thought. Tomorrow is not going to happen. A gaggle of rubberneckers watch me through a window.

"THAT'S IT, WATCH ME DIE, MOTHERFUCKERS."

Tania bullies them into moving, and Louis leaps down the steps into the snow, picks me up like a sack of potatoes, and eases me onto my little yellow bed. My lips are purple, skin covered in goosebumps. I mumble and shiver. I've been kicked off my throne by a fucking little angel. Tania is a fucking asshole; she won't let me crawl back up to the coke lines. Framed by the door, Raphael Gouin looks at me in sad sympathy.

"Quit looking at me, asshole."

I'm going to die slumped in the corner of this room, unloved and alone. Fuck. Don't do this to me, Jeff. Don't replace me with some other girl. Please, Jeff, call me. Call me and we'll talk like we used to. Please, Jeff. Love me. Please.

Out of nowhere a mouthful of water assaults my throat, and I throw up all over the carpet. I've got puke all over my mouth, my hands, even in my hair. Tania is trying to wipe me off, but I shove her away.

"This is just like with Martin. Don't you get it?"

"No."

"Yes, Philly. The same damn thing. You're heartbroken, and you're getting trashed to cope. What am I supposed to do with you?"

"It's not my fault. It's fucking Angelica who fucked everything up."

"Philly, you have to let go of him."

"Why is he leaving his job — *for her*? Why now? Why is he cooking, fucking, going out *with her*? Why isn't he with me? Why wasn't I good enough for him?"

"You're not the problem, Philly. The both of you together just weren't a good match. You deserve better than that."

"No. I can't live without him, Tan. I can't stop thinking about him. I daydream about us having kids together, all sorts of things. Why is bitch Angelica fucking slut getting what I deserve?"

I throw up again and we start all over …

Dawn tastes bitter. Submerged in a scalding bath, I look up at the grey sky and the thousand snowflakes that are falling. I peel off the layers of makeup and dried vomit. Someone is doing dishes in the kitchen.

The bungalow has turned into a garbage dump. My wet hair drips quietly onto the floor. Raphael is zipping up his coat. For once, he doesn't seem to be smiling. I should say something …"Thanks."

"What?"

"The dishes."

"No prob."

"Where are you going?"

"I told you. I'm going skating with the Nitrate boys."

"Oh, yeah. Have … fun."

"Have a nice day, Philomena."

He's wearing a big green toque, warm; it'll protect him from the storms. I can't do that — take care of myself, be smart. I stare at him, open mouthed, my eyes on his, a line of drool coming out of the corner of my mouth.

"You okay …? Philomena?"

"Huh?"

"Are you okay?"

"No."

"You … uh, want to come skating? Get … out of here, I mean?"

"I don't have skates."

"We'll figure something out."

"I don't have a boyfriend, either. I'm so sad I want to die."

"We can figure that out, too."

The farmhouse sits huge and alone in the middle of the white field, old grey boards scored by the seasons, the sun and rain. An old building still managing to stay standing despite the weather. The field is surrounded by huge evergreens carrying great loads of snow. He parks in front of a small house with yellow shingles. Raphael invites me inside, opening the door without knocking. Smells like Mom's cooking — someone else's mom's cooking — and a great big Labrador is sleeping next to the crackling fire.

"My baby's home!"

A tiny woman with huge hips bounds over to Raphael to take him in her arms and pat at his belly.

"I made meatloaf! Can finally put some meat on your little bones!"

"Thanks, Mom. Is Phil here, yet?"

"Nope. Late, as usual. You going to introduce me to your friend, baby?"

"Ah, right. This is Philomena. Philomena, this is Diana, my mom."

She wraps me up with her strong arms.

"My god! Can't Montreal feed you kids? You're all so skinny! Please, sit, I made some pea soup. Would you like some coffee, dear?"

Diane hands me a cup with Garfield painted on its side as a hulking bearded man steps into the house with a load of chopped wood in his arms. The Lab gets to its feet, tail wagging, tongue sloppy with drool. Happy doggo.

"Mr. Artiste has arrived, eh?"

Raphael greets his father, and the door opens yet again for Philippe, six foot and all smiles, with a gravelly voice and smiling eyes. The whole family hugs, kisses, talks over each other. I am a bug scurrying across the floor, trying to stay out of sight. After more introductions, we sit at the table, and my stomach starts to lurch. Philippe asks me what I do for work.

"I'm a beautician in a funeral house."

The breadbasket stops midair in Raphael's hands.

"But right now I'm between jobs. Just came back from Toronto."

"What were you doing there?"

"I … uh … was training with live models."

"C'mon, you like 'em dead or alive? You gotta choose one."

Everyone laughs. Raphael calls Philippe a dumbass. "Live models are nude, Phil."

"Nah! For real? You drew guys nekkid?"

"Women, too."

"Well, hell! I'm going to Tronno, too!"

Everyone thinks it's funny. Everyone but me.

"Yeah, well, good luck. It killed my relationship and all my dreams. It's a high price to pay just to see someone naked."

Papa Gouin clears his throat and turns the conversation around.

"What's new with you, big guy?"

Raphael's eyes light up with something almost holy when he starts telling them about Nitrate's success. His sudden excitement captivates me; I didn't know he could be so amazingly enthusiastic, so passionately hungry.

"We're sending out feelers to start a media platform. Opportunities have been cropping up for a few years, and we'd be crazy not to take a shot. I want to help people get exposed to new stuff, work that's really experimental."

Philippe, mouth full of mashed potatoes, laughs in his face.

"You coulda just stayed here and worked in construction like the rest of us?"

"Raph is good at other things, Phil. Come on."

"Stop defending him, Ma. He's just wasting his life."

"Phil, c'mon. I'm not wasting my life. I'm doing something I love, and it's going really —"

"I never seen you on TV, Raph …"

"I'm not on TV, Phil. I do shorts and web videos."

"You don't make no sense, since you moved to Montreal."

"We're just different people. It's all good."

"How different, Raph? Your fruity movie carnivals are making you a fucking fag."

Fork and knife bounce off my plate. Every eye turns to me.

"Nitrate is an amazing festival. If Raphael hadn't created it, my friend Daniel would never have seen his dreams come true, Tania wouldn't have gotten me out of my dad's house, and I would, no joke, be lying dead, today. I'm living proof that the world needs hope. And that's what your brother gives people."

Diane hands me an old pair of skates hidden away in a closet. She kneels to help me tie the laces up. A real mom.

"Thanks for what you said, earlier. I love that boy, but I don't really know what it is that he does in Montreal. What you said about hope back there, that meant a lot to me. It's none of my business, but let me give you a little word of wisdom. There's nothing better for a bruised heart than a little fresh air and sunshine."

She puts Raphael's old toque on my head. I look like a bright Golden Delicious.

Fat flakes of snow fall through the trees down on the beaver dam holding the lake in. Raphael falls on his ass trying to be a figure skater; everyone laughs but me. I'm stunted, can't enjoy the moment. He joins me where I'm standing alone and offers me his arm while we skate together.

"Thanks for what you said about Nitrate."

"Thanks for bringing me up here."

"You're a mysterious one, you know."

"What do you mean?"

"Are you, like, obsessed with death?"

I smile for the first time all day. A breathy laugh even manages to escape.

"Pretty fucked fixation to have, eh?"

"A little, yeah."

"I don't know. I like to honour the dead … It's hard to explain. I think that since the dead can't do or say anything anymore, don't have a say over what happens anymore, they deserve to at least be buried looking their best."

He looks at me admiringly; I can see myself shrinking under his gaze.

"You're a really special girl, Philly Flynn."

My goddamn oversized skates trip me up, and I fall flat on my face.

"But you skate like shit."

Before Nitrate's closing night, Raphael drops me off at a hair salon. Authentique Aesthetique: exactly what I need. I ask the lovely Carole to cut my hair short. Very short.

"You sure, honey? We could do some layers —"

I'm done being Sleeping Beauty. Time to become a Bond girl. Time to make Dad proud.

14

Marseille, April 2017

The sun sets in the port, packed with boats. I'd cry with joy, if I weren't too proud. The sails slap in the wind. The smell of the sea is everywhere. I haven't felt this good in nine years. It's probably because of the massive backpack I'm carrying with me.

I get lost in the streets around the Pharo Palace. Eventually, I make it back to the shore and find Sylvain's restaurant, Chez Michel. I can see him wearing a classic sailor costume, pushing a mop around in the big front windows. After a bottle of white wine and seafood spaghetti, we get to the updates.

"How're my kids?"

"Great! Louis won a prize for his short, and Tania's working too much. She's moved up to communications assistant."

"Of course she is. When she wants something, nothing gets in her way, just like her mom."

"Yeah."

"Have you seen Manon lately?"

"Nope. All I know is that she hates the condo — too small."

"No kidding. Considering how big our house was, it's no surprise that her sardine can drives her crazy."

"Yeah …"

Please get back together and move into your big old house that smelled like bacon and buttered toast on Sunday mornings. Please. I want to go back to being seven years old and fall asleep in the mint-green armchair.

"How about you, Philly-bee? You doing okay?"

"Not really. I didn't know where to go."

"Well, I'm glad you came. The sea's good for the soul, you'll see. You can stay in my condo. I'm taking care of my mom's place. She's in Corsica until the end of summer."

"You sure? I don't want you to —"

"Come on. This is perfect. Well, the apartment is small, I'm warning you. And very old."

"It'll be great. Perfect for what I need."

"Stay as long as you like, honey."

"Thanks, Sylvain."

I get my groceries at the Casino supermarket, smiling ear to ear like I'd never bought food on my own before. I fill the fridge with fruit, cheese, and wine; I fill the breadbox with baguettes. Stare out at the ocean from Sylvain's sofa, sing Serge

Gainsbourg until my throat is raw, do crosswords on the beach, tan, fall back in love with reading. Just fucking reading! I finish *Frida: The Story of Her Life* by Vanna Vinci — a graphic novel that manages to jump-start my creativity. My fingers burn to draw something. I need paintbrushes.

"It was neither man nor beast."

The Creature and the Woman are aching to come to life, so I burn through the nights in a trance.

I draw and write for hours without stopping; I just can't stop. My inspiration takes over so completely that I forget to eat. Luckily, Sylvain swings by after closing the restaurant and feeds me leftover bouillabaisse. Eating gives me energy but brings me back to reality. My back hurts from working seated on the floor.

"When the Woman's scarred lips met her lover's beautifully barbed mouth, he brushed off the blood he drew with as-yet-unseen kindness. When it saw her limping gait, it carried her in its tireless arms. It made her purr with pleasure. They were happy. Nothing could ever tear them apart."

I set up a web of string in the apartment and pin all my sketches to it. There are hundreds of drawings hanging in the air between the walls of Sylvain's apartment. I have several drawings of the Shadow Kingdom, but none are quite sombre enough. Soon, though. Sinister old men, pallid eunuchs, and sacrificed virgins move with life as the breeze blows overhead.

* * *

I leave the apartment for the first time in a week, maybe more. Ink stains all over my hands, and I have to hide my bloodshot eyes behind big dark sunglasses to keep from going blind in the daylight. On the terrace at the Italian, I order spaghetti and a beer. Ever my father's daughter. The line rings three times, and he picks up.

"Why ... hello, Philly."

"Did I wake you up?"

"It's fine."

"How are you?"

"Still ... not ... dead."

"Dad!"

"Kidding."

"Seriously. You okay?"

"Sure ... am."

"I can come back if you need."

"Is that ... the sea ... in the background?"

"It is. It's amazing. You'd love it here. It's really doing me a lot of good."

"That's great, Philly. You ... having fun?"

"Yeah. I'm working on something. A book, maybe, I think."

"I always knew ... you'd do ... something great."

"I don't know if it'll be any good."

"Yeah, well ... that's life ... right?"

"Right."

"What's the title?"

"It doesn't have one yet."

"It could be … *Papa Flynn, King of Connemara*."

"It could. Why not. How's the chemo going?"

"The nurses … are sweet."

"That's good. I miss you, Daddy."

"Me, too, baby."

"If you need me to come back …"

"No, no. Keep … writing. I'm going to … strut on down to … the chemo shop. My daughter, a writer! How about that!"

He asks me if I need any money, and I lie so he doesn't worry. A two-year-old at the next table blows bubbles in his juice. It goes all over the place, onto the tablecloth, making his mom angry. Will Dad ever be a grandfather? Will time be on our side? The urge to draw comes over me again, and I rush back to the apartment.

"Some impossible magic took root in the Woman's womb. A liquid egg grew in the heat of her body. While hope for a royal heir beamed across the Kingdom of Shadows, the Creature was gnawed at by the fear of eventually being erased. *You will always be in my heart*, the Woman promised it in a whisper. But the Creature withdrew within itself, suddenly threatened by its partner's boundless happiness. The more the egg grew within her, the smaller the Creature began to feel. Burning with a terrible fever, she refused all care, awaiting the death she felt in the Creature's bitterness."

You will always be in my heart.

I scramble some eggs in a pan without any seasoning. What is he doing, right now? I crush the yoke with villainous pleasure. I have to forget. I have to move on.

"Weak, its skin falling off in sloughs, the Creature slid over the sodden earth with empty eyes. The Woman would give birth soon, heralding the Creature's own demise. Sliding through the mud, the terrible Onyx Serpent approached. *Sire, Sire, do my eyes betray me? Has your strength abandoned you? Do not worry so, for there is no need. Allow me to dispel this hex cast upon you. Simply perform the rite granting me the soul of that thing that causes you such pain, and together we shall regain our kingdom.* The pact signed in blood, the Serpent fed its venom into the Creature, who, struck by a death-like forgetting, crawled back to the castle, its eyes blind to love."

The wind pricks every inch of my exposed skin; I should have worn a jacket, shouldn't have left the apartment so quickly, but the full moon glowed so beautifully on the water that I didn't stop to think. Mrs. Jorish had a cassette recording of the sea, and she loved falling asleep while listening to it, rocked to sleep by the sound. The waves filled her bedroom while I watched over her last moments, her long fingers and fading memories threaded through mine. She passed taking a deep breath, calm, almost smiling. This art project that's giving me the strength to live is dedicated to her. I see the title spelled out for me in a crash of Mediterranean seafoam.

"In Your Human Hands."

15

Marseille, June 2017

My short hair is sun bleached and my freckles have come back. Raphael's mom was right. I'm on my way back from the Plage des Catalans, towel around my neck, flip flops in my hand. I go to unlock the door, but it's already open. It can't be — I had locked it. I'm sure.

"Sylvain?"

No answer. Please, Mrs. Jorish, watch over me. The floorboards creak like old bones. Half my drawings have been taken off their strings, goddamn it. Please, don't let my manuscript be gone, please … fuck. There's someone in the kitchen … some maniac is burning my book in the kitchen.

"Surprise!"

Tania leaps on me, and we fall to the floor, laughing like little girls. We settle in the living room and sip milky pastis together. Tania, surprisingly animated despite her jet lag, gives me the latest news. "I was working like crazy. My boss was so fucking clueless that I started breaking out from the stress. It got so bad that I had insomnia for *months*. And for what? I really had to ask myself, *Why am I killing myself for fucking yogurt ads?* So, I quit."

"Really?"

"Yup. I said, 'Fuck it.' I want to travel, create, live, have *experiences*. I don't want to stay fucking stuck in a damn office."

"Wow. Pretty brave."

"Just doing like you, Philly. Everyone's got to get out of their shitty situations themselves. I'm not going to die in a shitty job waiting for my boyfriend to come back home. Since Daniel started working at the NFB, we never fuck anymore. I think the last time we fucked was two months ago. Two months. That isn't fucking normal. Is it normal?"

I fill my glass and rest my head on her shoulder.

"I'm really happy you're here, Tan."

"Me, too. I was a little surprised by how you decorated, though ..."

"Yeah, I kinda went a little nuts."

"I found the manuscript in my dad's room."

"You didn't read it, did you?"

"A bit."

"No!"

"Relax, Philly. It's really good."

"I don't know … I'm just goofing around …"

"What do you mean, *goofing*? You're writing a real graphic novel."

"Well, I don't know. Maybe not a graphic novel …"

"A graphic fairy tale, a dark fairy tale."

"It's weird …"

"No, it's refreshing. It's different."

"Yeah? You think it might be okay?"

"For sure. How does it end?"

"That's my problem … I don't know … how it ends. I never know how to fucking end anything."

Tania flicks her lighter and takes a slow drag. Memories of autumn rain and ruddy skin come back to me.

"Have you talked to Jeff?"

"No."

"So? How do you feel?"

"Better. Really good."

"Good. Have you been laid since you got here?"

"No."

"Philly."

"I hadn't even thought of it. I swear, Tania, it's like I just came out of a coma. I don't know … It's like …"

"Like what?"

"I don't know if I'm going to be able to fall in love again. I wanted to fucking die! For a guy that I was only with for six months! Makes no fucking sense. I feel like I have a hole inside me that won't close. Pretty stupid, eh?"

"Not stupid. Just give yourself some time. Have a little fun in the meantime. It'll help that hole shut itself."

I'm not so sure that my Frankenstein heart can be fixed. But I hope you're right, Tania.

To mark Tania's arrival in Marseille, her dad offers a friend's sailboat for a trip along the inlets off the coast. It's the tippiest boat in France. When dawn rises, breaking the endless line of the horizon, it literally takes my breath away. I sleep like a baby, gently rocked by the swells of the Mediterranean, and wake up red as a lobster. We jump into the waves like little girls the second we throw anchor. I feel that deep vertigo looking down into the water below. One time, with the boat berthed in Cassis, we set up two little tents in a pine forest. Tania and I catch the last rays of the sun while Sylvain lights a campfire. I put my feet in the sand and soak up the thousand shades of blue, finding new meaning in the colours.

Just before going to sleep, Tania can't stop farting, and it smells like death. I laugh until I pee a little. Just like the good old days.

My feet are back on solid ground, my head full of the sapphire sky.

Daily life in Marseille is steady and free: laze around on the beach, go to the theatre and museums, listen to Sylvain tell us stories of his youth, and drink Picon and beer while watching the sun set. Vacationing with my best friend in the south of France is bliss, and I soak up every second. The last time we travelled together was in Argentina. Ten years ago I was the very definition of *virgin*. Now, I feel heavy with the weight in my heart. What matters is that Tania is here. She'll always be there for me. Her strength pushes me on. I hope she can see that.

"Marketing director for an airline — that sounds great! What do you think? If I can't travel around with my workaholic boyfriend, I'll make sure that my friends can travel in style. Should I apply? Fuck it, I just did."

While Tania scours job listings, I work on "In Your Human Hands" with a warmth inside me that grows every day.

"Hidden in the undergrowth like a shadow hiding from a flame, the Creature stalked toward the royal bedchamber. Drunk with venom, its soul numbed, it no longer recognized the Woman and, right when her birth pains were about to begin, it threw itself at her swollen belly and slashed at her entrails. While giving the killing blow to its would-be heir, the Creature saw with horror that the Woman still looked at it with love. *We were two crazy monsters to have believed*, she thought. Not knowing how to hide from those eyes, the Creature tore them out with a single stroke of its claws."

"Tan, look — I've tweaked the Creature …"

"Oh, that's a familiar face …"

"You think he'll recognize himself?"

"You think he'll actually read it?"

No, of course not. Either way, I'm not set on the design, but I have to keep sketching, and I know his face by heart.

* * *

We celebrate the beginning of summer at a bar with a view of the entire city. A satin shirt takes me by the hips and fills my ear with Spanish whispers. Blushing like a tomato, I let myself be led in a very slow dance. A big black guy in a tiny T-shirt licks Tania's neck. She gives herself over completely, and I start to feel uncomfortable. What Tania wants, she gets. She lets him touch her ass, her face, her breasts. I can't help but think of Daniel, and I step on my dance partner's foot. I apologize clumsily. I need a second. Disappointed, he leaves to dance with the next girl he sees.

I step away from the crowd and let my gaze drift over the city. Three months ago, I would have jumped off the balcony and dashed my head on the stone sidewalk. Today, I have a graphic novel to finish.

A guy lights a cigarette next to me. Tall and thin. Perfectly tanned, curly blond hair frames his face. Le Petit Prince. He smokes Gauloises, too — my favourite. They smell good, and I have to look away. Shit, he's offering me one.

"Uh … no, thanks. Well … okay, yeah. Why not?"

"Cute accent … Where are you from?"

"Montreal."

"Ah, Quebec. Looks like a charming place to be."

"Yeah. Depends. You? You live here?"

"I was born in Paris, in fact, but my mother has a *pied-à-terre* here, and I've been coming for visits since I was a child. She has remarried and all that bother. My father lives in Saint-Martin. Indescribable. Have you ever been?"

"No, not yet."

"I would rather like to take you there."

"No kidding!"

I like this face, so soft and pure. The Mediterranean's rhythm casts its magic over us.

"I've always adored the sea. I took sailing lessons when I was sixteen, and I do so love to sail. When life becomes too much, I set out for the sea. It truly is the best remedy."

"You know a lot for someone so young."

"You think I'm young? How old do you think I am?"

"I don't know … you look like a kid."

"That's because I take after my mother. I'm not a child after all; I'm twenty years old."

I laugh out loud and start walking down the fire escape. The nicotine is making me dizzy.

"Where are you going, Miss Montreal?"

"I'm going for a walk."

"Might I keep you company?"

"So long as I don't have to change your diaper along the way."

"Who knows, ma'am? I might be the one who will have to change your diaper."

His name is Charli Campana. He studies architecture at the Sorbonne, vacations in Marseille, and goes to the islands to visit his father a few times a year. A kind of teenage dream. We sit on the rocks, dangle our feet over the void, and he devours me with his every look.

"I'm too old for you," I say.

He slides my hair behind my ear, brushes my cheek with his hand, and runs his fingers along my lips until he finally kisses me.

"Terribly sorry. I simply couldn't help myself."

I bite his lips softly until he puts his hand on the back of my neck and kisses me until I can't breathe. I'm both predator and prey and don't feel guilty for a second.

"A widdle kiddy! Yay!" Tania dances around happily, and I snort and giggle like a little girl. My lips are swollen, and my neck is covered with hickeys.

"Friend him on Facebook."

"No, no way. Honestly, that would be so stupid. Except … but, it could be … No, bad idea. What happens on vacation has to stay on vacation. What did I get out of friending Eamonn? Nothing. All it did was make me realize how I wasn't special at all. And you … did you sleep well?"

"What's the real question, Inspector Flynn?"

"Did you cheat on Daniel with the guy yesterday?"

A flock of seagulls leaps on a French fry cone. Hungry birds make a lot of racket.

"No. We made out, and he fingered me for a few seconds in the taxi. I … I just couldn't do it. I'm so fucking pissed."

"Why? That's sweet, isn't it?"

"It isn't good at all. Love turns me into a pussy. If Daniel can't satisfy my basic needs, it just makes sense that I get what I need elsewhere, no? Anyway … and I still felt guilty, you know? I felt so guilty that I wanted to message him something cute, a heart or something like that … But I couldn't even do it. I can't cheat on him, and I can't write to tell him that I love him. Fucking pathetic! The worst part is … it's even been a while since we've fought."

"That's good, isn't it?"

"I don't know."

Le Petit Prince sends me a friend request.

I'm nervous, my hands are dripping, and my throat is dry. I'm so stupid. The tall, narrow house is on a paved road flanked by stone stairways that I climb, so terrified that my pits are sweating. What the hell am I doing? He's too young. We were drunk last time. Lightning doesn't strike twice.

"Good evening, Philomena."

"Hey. Good day, uh, good evening, Charli."

"You are simply ravishing."

"Really? Thanks. It's an old dress. No, that's not true. I just bought it. I don't know why I said that. You're pretty, too. I mean — your shirt is pretty. Is it linen?"

That's a bad sign. I should really go, get back to writing. I'm going to make up an excuse and leave, say that my stomach's upset.

"Would a glass of wine suit you?"

"Okay."

We have our drinks in the living room. A local rap album plays in the background. I don't like it, but I pretend to because that's how my mother raised me.

"I would so like to see Canada one day, see real snow."

"It's as pretty in real life as in the pictures, but after six months of cold, ice, and slush, you can really get sick of it.

"What is slush?"

"It's snow. It's greyish-brown and wet. More a gel than a liquid. It's disgusting."

We really don't have anything to talk about, to be honest. I'm going to leave. He lights a cigarette and offers me the pack. His long fingers brush against mine. Okay. Just one.

"The way you speak is fascinating. I only understand every other word."

"Sorry. I'll try to be more careful."

"Anything but! I find it terribly sexy."

I should really go. If I stay, in two minutes I'm going to find myself naked in the arms of this baby boy, my cigarette burning his mommy's sofa. Except the more I tell myself to go, the more my legs relax. My panties are as wet as when I was jerking Pierre-Luc Dion off. Fuck. Le Petit Prince turns me on. Okay. I'm going to have to get a hold of myself. I am a grown woman. I can do this. I'm going to get up, say goodbye in a strong, dignified voice, and leave politely. Okay. No problem. I open my mouth and what comes out? "Is there any more wine?"

The world crashes around us. A flick of his wrist and my dress in on the floor, my nipple in his mouth. Completely powerless, I let him go down on me like he's digging for treasure. I knew I'd ruin the damn sofa.

"Ready for the entree?"

We break open freshly caught lobster and dip the soft flesh in lemon and chive sauce.

"At your age I was eating Kraft Dinner with hot dog wieners."

"I can't take any credit for it. My auntie taught me all of this. Also, the seafood is incredibly fresh here. Completely smashing."

"So you sail, you cook well, you're an amazing kisser … do you have *any* flaws?

"I do: I'm young."

We fuck all night long. Amazing youth. Maybe he's actually right? Our ages aren't all that far apart. He fucks me on the kitchen counter, in the shower, on the living room carpet, in his bed. Where would we live? Here? I guess I've always dreamed of a stone house with white shutters in the country … Goddamn it. I'm starting to fall, again. I have to stop this. But no, he gets hard again in all of three seconds and leaves his mark on every part of my body. He never stops. *An author and her young lover lived next to the sea — happily ever after.* It sounds like a dream, but a beautiful dream. For once.

* * *

A light breeze dances through the bedroom curtains. Resting on his chest, I never want to get up, leave the room, his arms. Charli and his golden curls; Charli who makes me smoke in bed.

"Do you have any plans?"

"Staying glued to you for the rest of my life. That work?"

"It does for me."

"Charli, are you an angel?"

"If I am an angel, you must be a fairy."

He makes me an espresso. I hate it, but I pretend to like it because it's so cute that he dotes on me. I even take a picture and post it on Instagram to show him how much I appreciate his making me a coffee. My phone lights up with a dozen missed calls from my mom. My voice mail is full.

"Sorry, Charli. I have to call my mom. I think it's important."

He kisses me on the back of my neck, sending me into a stupor. I wait until he's in the shower to dial the number.

"Philomena! Finally. Oh my god! I've been trying to reach you all day!"

The panic in her voice shatters my sexual seaside reverie. If she's bugging me just to complain about fucking Raymond, I'm going to hang up on her. She doesn't say a word. I can only hear Yappy whining in the background.

"What's going on, Mom?"

"It's your father."

"What about Dad?"

It had better not be her bitching about his fucking alimony payments again. Fucking Raymond never stop talking about it. Too shy to admit your boyfriend's on your ass, Ma?

"Mom, say something."

"Your father is dying, Philomena. You have to come back. I … I can't do this alone. I can't. His doctor called me … he has a week … oh my god. I don't know what to do, Philomena …"

There is an otherwise perfect circular ring that a coffee cup has left on the counter. It is round and black. There is a round, black coffee stain on the counter.

"I'm so sorry, bunny. So sorry …"

My phone shatters into a thousand pieces when it hits the ground.

In the shower, Charli hums a timeless French piece, one of Piaf's love ballads.

16

Somewhere on the South Shore, June 2017

I emptied out his apartment and put his clothes in boxes for donation. All that's left is a cardboard box full of memories: pictures, my childhood drawings, birthday cards that I had drawn for him, his collection of VHS tapes and the machine with it, his Brigitte Bardot poster, carefully rolled up. Mom offered to help, but I told her not to. Dad wouldn't have wanted her going through his stuff. I check the apartment one last time before going to hide in the old Tercel.

I was twelve years old when my dad came to pick me up from the apartment Mom shared with her Cuban boyfriend. Dad was all puffed up and proud of his new car. At the time I hoped that he would buy a shiny red Sunfire coupe. I thought a Pontiac Sunfire was the definition of sexy. My teenage heart fell when he parked the tiny, funny-smelling turquoise Toyota. Today, the car smells like cigarette smoke and spaghetti sauce. It smells like him.

In the hospital's palliative care wing, I found a deflated balloon tied to the bed. It took me a second to recognize him. Thinking of putting makeup on his slack, colourless face made me want to jump from the ninth-storey window. I held on to the bed with all my might. "The treatments have unfortunately not had the desired effect," the doctor said. I sat by the bed for hours before he came out of his confused sleep. He was too proud to let himself cry in front of me, but his lips trembled, and his hand reached around desperately for mine. I broke down.

"I'm so sorry I wasn't there for you, Daddy. I'm so sorry I left you all alone. It's all my fault. If I had just been there for you …"

"If you … had been … here … it would … have happened … anyway."

"I'm not going anywhere, Daddy. I'm back and I'm here for you. You'll have whatever you need. I love you."

"I … love … you … too … Philly."

I snuffle down a box of Timbits with strawberry filling in the Tim Hortons parking lot. Dad used to call them "little Yeti nuts." He had a way of making the mundane funny, of calling things by a different name, of making my imagination take off.

"Us Flynns, our ancestors were Irish warriors, did you know that, Philly?"

"Uh-huh."

"Did I ever tell you about my cousin, Lucky?"

"Who?"

"You know the little elf on the cereal box? Lucky Charms. That's him."

"The little guy dressed in green, he's your cousin?"

"Absolutely. On your grandmother's side."

"He's still alive?"

"Of course."

"Can I meet him?"

"Sure, you can, but you'll have to really pay attention. He's pretty small, and he likes to hide in clover fields. If you look carefully, you'll be able to see him."

Daddy, are you in heaven?

I always thought he'd live forever, like those heroes who get shot a million times and never give up the ghost. Why isn't life more like a movie?

Like *Diamonds Are Forever*, my favourite James Bond movie. How many times did we act out the shootout in the pool, he and I? I dressed up as Tiffany Case when I was ten years old. She was the villain but turned around in the end. Dad bought me a red wig on Saint-Hubert, and Mom lent me her old pink negligee.

"Wouldn't you rather have a nice witch costume?"

Fuck, no. No one recognized my costume, and I couldn't care less. Dad and I, we knew.

"Philly?"

"Yes? Are you thirsty, something hurt? Do you need something, Daddy?"

"Get me … out … of here."

We spent the last few hours of his life together happily making as many of his dreams come true as possible. No more hospital. The first thing he wanted was to get *007* tattooed over his heart.

"Really? You always say that tattoos are for little ghetto bums."

"They … are. And I … want … a big … one."

In a tattoo parlour on Ontario, a busty woman with long purple hair made his dream come true. I did the same, like a permanent father-daughter BFF. Side by side, we etched ourselves with the memories we've shared forever. His face screwed up with pain, but he didn't complain at all. And he stepped out of the shop with a smile shining like the sun.

The city is dark, and I have a diamond tattooed to the inside of my forearm.

The highway licks the Tercel's undercarriage, faceless fields roll by, untouched sheds slowly disintegrate; brown and black-and-white cows dot the horizon. The Ottawa river never lets us down. We're going home, Daddy.

I place his charcoal drawing on the shelf above the wood-fired stove.

"I always ... wanted to be ... an artist ... too."

My dad never ceases to amaze.

"When I was small, I saw ... a painting ... Armand Vaillancourt, you know? Really ... impressive. I would have ... loved to ... to try."

We made our way to a studio on d'Iberville, and it was almost impossible to get the wheelchair and oxygen tank into the dilapidated elevator. Liam Albanese, my old classmate, met us in his huge loft studio.

"Welcome to my new gallery. Please, make yourself at home, Mr. Flynn."

Impressed by how out-of-the-way the place is, my dad is thoroughly charmed. He paints for thirty minutes before the pain leaves him paralyzed. He falls asleep, a wilted king on the sofa, his cheeks hollow, his skin like moss. Liam digs up a wool blanket for my dad and a bottle of red for me. No need for a glass. I step up to the easel and draw my dad the way he lives in my imagination: a man with striking eyes, flanked by mythical Irish mountains.

The sun sets in the middle of the lake, a great tired orange rolling over the horizon. When his parents died he inherited this cabin on Flynn Lake, lost in the great Pontiac forest. And I was the next one on the list, the next inheritor. I remember summers past when my dad taught me how to fish, and I would come back to town covered in mosquito bites, which made my mother scream. Tania came with us one time, during high school summer vacations. This is where we smoked our first cigarettes and stuffed ourselves with marshmallows, where my dad taught us how to debone perch. Now the cabin on Flynn Lake is all that I have left of him. A kitchen with three cupboards and a small table, a closet-sized bathroom, and a loft with two narrow bedrooms and a sofa. The sofa. Fuck. Jeffrey is the only guy I ever brought here, the only guy I ever fucked in my dad's cottage. I can't stand it.

The suede loveseat glimmers in the wild twilight. The grass on the bank is higher than ever, the dock looks ready to fall apart, and the balcony is rotting. It's going to take real heart to spruce the place up, but the timing's shit. I don't think I have any heart left.

"I will die hard ... or I won't die ... at all," he said. After pretending to be artists together, Dad and I went to eat two big bloody steaks with a bottle of red wine.

"Stop at ... at the convenience ... store."

"What do you need?"

"Du Maurier ... king size ..."

"What the hell, Dad."

"You won't deny ... me ... my last ... requests."

I shredded the rib-eye into tiny pieces so I could spoon them into his mouth. Three minuscule bites and that was it. I had to hold his cigarette for him, the nerves in his fingers totally shot. After throwing up bile, he handed me a letter addressed to my mom.

"There are ... lots of things ... I wanted ... to say ... but ..."

"I'll give her the letter, Daddy. I promise."

"You know, Philly ... living in fear ... means giving up ... on happiness. Never ... never forget ... that."

Nothing is left of the fucking loveseat. It burned up in great billows of black smoke, even the springs melted into nothingness in the fire. Barefoot on the wet grass, eyes lost in the thousand stars above, I'm looking for a sign so badly that my brain nearly explodes. Do the dead really go up to heaven? Did you meet Mrs. Jorish, Daddy? How am I supposed to live without you?

The toads croak so loud that I can't even hear myself think.

17

The Outaouais, August 2017

Twenty-seven years old and no one to celebrate with. I end up in the village bar in the middle of the afternoon. I order a pitcher of Rickard's Red and some vodka-pickle shots in honour of the good old days.

"No pickles here, lovey. Got pickled eggs, if you want."

I change tack and down one, two, three tequilas in a row. Even the boonies have lemons and salt.

Two months with no human contact. I haven't been able to leave our forest since my father's death. Too scared to go back to town, to reality. Here, no one pisses me off. I just float by with my ghosts. The fucker didn't even come to my dad's funeral. The bartender, who must have put on her makeup on the truck ride over, takes pity on me.

"What are you doin' here, gettin' drunk in the middle of nowhere? All alone, too."

"The world is fucked, lady. I'd rather hide in the woods. It's less dangerous."

"Where's your cottage?"

"Flynn Lake. Inherited it from my dad."

"Oh, I'm so sorry, honey."

"Cheers."

Half the pitcher runs down my chin and onto the floor.

"You're gonna throw up in my bar if you keep it up. You're too skinny to drink like a trout."

"I'm not too fucking small. I can drink."

I land on the floor with a splat like a sticky wet turd.

"Sorry … There are peanuts down here.

"Sit down. I'll make you some coffee."

"Nao. Imma … Imma go back …"

"Sit, I said! You can't drive. You're drunk as a skunk."

This bar sucks. It stinks, too, smells like the sixties brown all around. Fuck … I'm all alone. As lonely as can be. The bartender pulls me close; I think I might be crying.

"You can't stay here. I mean it, honey. When things get bad, you can't stay all alone at the edge of a lake. You gotta be with people who love you."

The wheels of the BMW crunch on the gravel, and high beams blind me. Tania gets out and jumps on me without shutting the car door. I cling to her like a koala.

"Happy birthday, Mowgli! Goddamn. When's the last time you took a shower?"

Louis cuts the engine. He gets out and stretches his whole body. He's finished the tattoo on his left arm. It's pretty, looks like a maze.

"Hey, kid. Look at what we brought you."

A McCain cake, completely demolished from bouncing along on the road. I've never been so happy in my life.

You're scaring us, Philly. Is there any *meat left on your bones?*

Louis makes us the biggest bonfire in history with what's left of the balcony. I tore it down myself. Tania heats spaghetti sauce, her dad's recipe, on the small stove in the cottage.

"I talked to my dad, yesterday. He sends you his love and wants me to tell you, you can go back to Marseille whenever you like."

"Thanks, but I don't have any money. Can't travel anymore."

"Come on. Your leave of absence has got to be about up, isn't it? You're going to go back to work, aren't you?"

"I don't know."

"Are you going to go back to Memorium? I mean … Considering what happened, it would make sense if you wanted a change …"

"How's your new job?"

"It's okay. But what's really great is the discount I get on international flights. So we'll be able to travel whenever we want."

"Great."

The sauce spits all over the kitchen and coagulates on the stove.

"How's your novel coming along?"

"Can we please talk about something besides me?"

"Okay. Dan and I went to a swingers' club."

"How was it?"

"So-so. We were looking for something we could do together."

"You two slept with other couples?"

"No, but I made out with a Brazilian, and I sucked Dan off on a kind of podium. People were watching. It was crazy."

"Weren't you scared?"

"No. It turned me on — I felt like a porn star. And Dan … he got so hard, Philly, it had been so long since I had seen him like that."

"Cool."

"We took GHB. I think that helped …"

"Yeah …"

She hands me a massively loaded plate of pasta and makes me a bib by tucking a dishcloth into my shirt. I can't even lift my fork off the table.

You have to go see a shrink, Philly … I'm scared that you're going to get cancer from keeping everything all locked up inside. Are you still hung up on Jeff? Why didn't you cry at the funeral?

Louis steps into the cottage, proud as a Boy Scout.

"Look, girls! The flames go all the way up to the sky!"

* * *

The Milky Way seems thicker than ever. Louis does a monologue on the constellations in the black; Tania puffs away at the joint impatiently but finally hands it over.

"If I had known that you'd be such a pain I never would have invited you."

"That's what you get for being too chicken to drive on country roads."

"I have fucking eye problems, Louis Reynier."

"You're full of shit."

The smoke tears at my dry throat. I spit on the wet grass, and we all laugh hysterically. Louis takes the joint back and pores over my tattoo.

"Weren't you scared of needles before?"

"Well, yeah ... I got over it."

"It's really pretty."

"Thanks."

"Why a diamond?"

Fucking idiot.

All the insects just *had* to choose this moment to go quiet. Thanks, guys.

"It's all I have left of him. A tattoo and a cottage on a lake. Crazy isn't it? I'm never going to see him or hear him cough again. I'm never going to laugh at his lame jokes. My dad is gone."

Tania's perfectly manicured hand weaves itself fiercely into mine. All my fingertips have been chewed raw and bloody.

"It might be cheesy, Philly, but I'm sure he's watching over you."

"He'll never read my book."

"For sure, he will. He's got a direct connection, like angels. He can see everything."

Time for Louis to start coughing.

"Fuck, sis. You wanna ease off?"

"Shut up, I'm being poetic. What I really mean is … you don't need to go through this alone. We're here for you, Philly. I'm here for you."

"I know."

"You have to get out of the woods, doll. If you don't, you'll end up growing a beard."

A thick white fog creeps slowly over the lake. Held up, held together by brother and sister, I cast my father into the lake. His ashes dance on the water, glowing in the shared light of the bonfire and the stars.

18

Montreal, August 2017

Time to kiss First Avenue and all its shitty memories goodbye: Tania and Daniel have just moved to a tiny studio apartment in one of downtown's tallest condo towers. Dan always loved the Theatre District's energy. Tania only gave in after seeing the building's amazing gym facilities.

"I hate working out, but I force myself to run forty-five minutes on the fucking treadmill. Every day. Why? I'm eating my emotions. I'm starting to get pudgy."

"Come on, Tan, you've got a body to die for."

"I wear a girdle, Philomena."

Daniel meets us in the living room with a bottle of rosé and his famous plantain canapés with black bean sauce. Tania thanks him with a kiss behind the ear and wants to sit between his legs, but he gets up right away to adjust the lighting, change the music, chop a little bit of coriander along the way. Someone's got the jitters. Tania, with her sad clown face, lights a joint in the balcony doorway. I wrap myself around her to comfort her. I miss my dead father. She misses her boyfriend, and he's still in the room. We both deal in different ways.

The walls in the apartment are all white, the floor made of concrete, the decoration very minimalist. Like a mortuary. I think I miss my job. Yeah. It really helped to have something to do.

Daniel lifts a glass and tells me grandly that he's waiting to hear back about financing for a second short film.

"If it goes through, we'll shoot it in the Rockies."

"Oh, wow. The West Coast. That's … that's nice."

Tania refills her glass up to the rim.

"It's really fucking far, that's what it is."

Her glass overflows, but Tania doesn't seem to care, like she'll go on filling her glass forever. Daniel's stuck cleaning up the mess.

"Don't start with that again. It'll just be a week, Tania."

"Plus pre-production, post-production, promos, festivals, your job at the NFB …"

"Just what is your problem?"

"My problem, Daniel, is that I'm single without any of the fucking freedom."

"What do you want me to fucking do? To stop working so that I can focus on your clit full-time?"

"Fuck you. If you like making grant requests so much, why don't you go down on the lady from the arts council?"

Their voices fade the more they yell; I've become an expert in tuning it out. Eight months ago we were snarling hyenas. You would claw at my skin, my throat in your mouth, plundering my entire body. I loved it so much that I … No. Fuck, no! Your savage lust disgusts me. Revolts me. I *need* it to repulse me.

"Dan? What kind of movie will it be?"

"Post-apocalyptic."

"If you need help with makeup, I can help. I'd love to go … I did stuff like that at school."

Are you fucking kidding me? I know you, Philomena. I know what you're thinking. We're not going to scour the Rocky Fucking Mountains just so you can find Jeffrey Hudon. You've got to stop running after the hurt.

Tania gets up from table with a crash. Daniel sighs in exasperation.

"What's going on? Are you angry?"

"No. I'm not hungry anymore. You two make me sick with your fucking projects."

My swimming lane is virtually empty, so I do two hundred lengths in less than an hour. I don't get out of the pool because my muscles hurt. I get out because I see my dad bobbing in the shallow end.

I visit bookstores, take down the names of publishing houses that look interesting, read up on graphic novels, realize that mine still isn't finished, and start to doubt whether or not it could ever interest an editor. Why is Jeff's life going so well while mine is such a failure?

Lost in the rows of graphic novels that were supposed to inspire me, I start to suffocate. An image of a hugely successful mastodon, sitting brilliantly on his throne, taunts me. The year's darling graphic novel is also about monsters. I'm going to set the bookstore on fire.

Rain falls on the marquees above Plaza Saint-Hubert. I'm soaked, freezing; I'll never be able to write something new. I'll never get published. I'm going to die alone, penniless.

The Memorium funeral home stands unmoving at the end of the street.

Daron Dimopoulos, the godfather of embalming since the dawn of time, paces endlessly in his potpourri-smelling office.

"All my sympathies for your daddy. Having known in advance, for example, we would have sent flowers, something. And, you know, if you had wanted to do it here, we would have offered a good price, because you are part of the family. You know that, yes?"

"Thank you, Mr. Dimopoulos. But we did it on the South Shore. Very intimate."

"You did makeup on him?"

"No, he wanted to be cremated."

"Ah. That's good. When will you come back? The new girl, she's not good. You're not just a technician, you are an artist! People can see it on our dead, trust me on that! I don't mean to rush you, no. No, you come back when you want. It would be nice as hell if it would happen fast, because everyone's in a race to die before the next one."

Sleepless on the sofa, the orange light bleeds through the blinds, drawing prison bars on me. What am I supposed to do with my life? "I have nothing for I no longer have him anymore," Frida wrote about Diego Rivera. She also said that he was the worst thing that ever happened in her entire life, even worse than the bus accident that made the rest of her life so painful.

The fear of being alone in the world.

Tania walks out of her room with swollen eyes, drags her feet to the couch, and collapses into my arms. I rock her into stillness.

"Don't make things worse again, okay, Philly?"

"Okay."

I can hardly breathe, but I'm still alive.

19

Montreal, September 2017

I work on my book on the corner of Amherst and De Maisonneuve, on a terrace that thinks it's a garden.

"Eternal night had sapped the Kingdom of Shadows of all its colour, the land had become dry once again, and the plaintive wailing of the dead had begun to haunt the empty dungeon beneath the castle. Nothing was left of the Woman. Her flesh had been devoured by vultures and the memory of her existence erased by venom. As the Onyx Serpent had promised, the Creature had regained all its might, and believing itself invincible stalked the oozing corridors without knowing what it was looking for, without knowing what it sought."

I lift my eyes from the Kingdom of Shadows only to meet those of Raphael Gouin, across the street. He wears a trendy cap and the same big glasses; his red beard has grown long. It looks good. He looks like a hirsute Irish sailor. I've always loved red-headed guys. Like Eamonn. I haven't stalked him on Facebook in a really long time. Last I heard, he was still with his wife. And he never, ever wrote me back. Raphael waves at me and practically runs across the street. We peck cheeks like old friends. I smell like fucking chlorine.

"Hey, Philomena! Happy to see you."

"Me, too."

"You look good."

"Yeah, I'm doing better. How about you?"

"Really busy! The media platform is just getting hotter. I love it. Are you putting an art show together?"

"I, uh ... no, I'm working on a graphic novel ... a fairy tale, actually."

"That's great. I'm happy you've found your groove."

His smile is contagious. I talk too fast, and before I even know I'm doing it, I invite him to sit down.

There's just a little spit of coffee grounds left in the bottom of my cup. I don't know how to keep the conversation going, I should have pretended to be busy and let him go on his way. True to form, Raphael breaks the silence.

"I heard through the grapevine that you were living at Daniel's place?"

"Yeah, but I have to find a new place. It's just ..."

"You've run out of money?"

"No, that's not it. It's … it's stupid."

"What?"

"I just don't want to live alone."

He puts his hand on mine and gives me his most sincere condolences for my father's passing. It's touching, but it makes me uncomfortable. And he can tell.

"Look, Philly, I don't want to be a creeper, but I live in a big three-bedroom in Hochelaga. I'd be more than happy to rent a room out to you. Rent, heating, and internet split between the three of us would cost peanuts."

"Three of us?"

"Yeah, I live with a girl from L'Isle-aux-Coudres. Her name is Marie-Christine. She's quiet, keeps to herself, super clean. I'm sure you'd get along. You can come and see the place this evening, if you like."

"Uh … okay, I'll think about it. Thanks, Raph."

"My pleasure."

"Sorry, I have to go. I have dead people to make pretty."

The workspace hasn't changed an inch. White, sterile, and silent as ever. A body lies under a white sheet, face nearly destroyed by the trauma, a skull that looks like ground beef. A brutal return to reality. The man in his fifties lived alone, shot himself in the head. A neighbour called the cops three days later. Three days.

I feel my blood run cold.

I send Raphael a text to ask what time I can see the apartment.

The apartment is dark and narrow, but the backyard is a piece of heaven. Climbing plants, hammock, big table for hosting guests. There's even a little garden, courtesy of Marie-Christine.

Raphael makes us tea while Tigger, the cat, rubs himself on my jeans and leaves them looking like shag.

"The last tenant wanted to get rid of Tigger, so I kept him. I can't bring myself to abandon a pet."

It's funny. My throat isn't itchy, and my eyes aren't leaking. But Mom always told me I was allergic to cats ... Right ...? Marie-Christine sweeps in like a storm, apologizing for being late. She sits down on the toilet and starts peeing without shutting the door.

"One of my kids' parents wanted to talk to me about their daughter's food sensitivities. Poor thing can't digest *anything*."

She washes up and shakes my hand.

"Hiya, I'm Marie-Christine. It's great to meet you! Raph has told me great things about you."

"Oh ... that's nice."

"So, you want to rent the third room? You'll see, living with Raph is really great. He's the best roommate I've ever had."

The way she looks at him bothers me. I know that look.

"Marie's exaggerating ..."

"No, I'm not."

And Marie-Christine is off, making a racket with the pots and pans.

"How about some *risotto ai funghi*, kiddies?"

I can't get a word out before she's warbling an Italian operetta. Raphael bursts out laughing, the cat starts crying, and the vent hood starts cranking away like a wheezing monster. Wow. Definitely won't die quiet and alone here.

"All right. I'll take the room."

Marie-Christine hoots with joy, and Raphael comes to his feet clapping. I put my cards on the table before they get carried away: I have to be able to come and go as I please, I don't lend my car, don't share my groceries, and absolutely no one is allowed in my room. Marie-Christine hums happily, and Raphael laughs into his beard.

"That's more like it, Miss Flynn."

They mob me with hugs. This is really a happy place. It'll take me out of my comfort zone.

20

I spent the morning embalming an octogenarian couple, a lovers' suicide pact with a barbiturate kiss. I started by injecting the missus with formaldehyde, an old school courtesy. Her face was stunningly serene, likely the result of their shared promise being kept and their love going unbroken for eternity.

Tonight, Tania and Daniel are going out to the swingers' club that they've apparently joined, Marie-Christine has gone back home for the weekend, and Raphael is spending the evening with a new squeeze. I'm alone and free to my own devices. Free and alone to celebrate the love-hate relationship I've had with myself for the past twenty-seven years.

It's so great to be able to masturbate without distraction while listening to Sigur Rós. The heat of the water pulls me out of myself in a smoke-like ballet. Coming in the bath is melancholic. The doorbell rings through the apartment. Fuck it, they'll just have to go away. I slide my pussy closer to the faucet, arch my back, but *fuck* the doorbell keeps ringing. I throw my bath robe on, wring it out. My night is ruined. I'm going to beat whoever's ringing the goddamn bell to death.

Raphael takes his snowy boots off in the hallway.

"Good thing you were home. I can't find my keys."

"Weren't you with Maya?"

"Maika."

"Maika, right."

"No — she stood me up."

"Huh? Why?"

"I don't know … I'm fucking sick of this. Another Valentine's Day with no valentine."

"Forget that. Everyone hates Valentine's Day."

"Had I known, I wouldn't have bought this …"

He pulls an enormous Laura Secord heart out of his backpack, full of tiny chocolates for a couple to share. It's hard not to laugh. How can such a creative guy fall into such lame clichés?

"You're really cute, Raph."

"Yeah, well … girls don't seem to like nice guys in real life …"

We drink mugs of wine in our pyjamas while watching *Moulin Rouge!* Satine dies in Christian's arms in a last loving embrace. Raphael sobs into my shoulder.

"I want to be with a woman like that."

"She's a whore, Raph."

"Yeah, but they love each other. Come what may, they love each other. Why can't I have something like that?"

"Because life isn't a movie. Real love and real death aren't terribly amazing when they aren't on a big screen."

"Yeah, normal as shit. I'm going to bed. Thanks for supper."

"Okay, no. I'm not going to let you slink away like a dying dog."

"That's not what I'm doing."

"Raphael Gouin, you're going to get dressed. You're my valentine tonight, and I'm taking you out."

The disco lights flash nonstop at Darling Bowling, and we play like morons. I buy him beer after beer, losing count, losing track. Working with dead people has got to mean I get to feel alive every now and then. We dance dirty in the middle of the bowling lane; a bunch of old men buy us a round of shots. Raph makes me laugh so hard I almost piss my pants. His glasses are falling off his face, his teeth glow in the black light, his testosterone crashes into my hormones. My obvious thirst for flesh triggers his own desire. He leans his body into mine, kisses me without asking, and we crumple to the floor while I wriggle around under his T-shirt.

"Hey! Kids! This isn't a motel."

We walk down rue Ontario with our jackets unzipped, looking for a secluded spot. His hands grab the frozen flesh of my ass behind a garbage Dumpster, and I jerk him off through his boxers while he sucks on my neck. His dick is nice and hard in my icy hands, a little patch of fur that warms my wrist. This is so crazy. I mean, it's Raph. A year ago, he was gallantly holding my hand on a snowy skating rink, and now he's fingering me in a back alley.

I flip my hair over my shoulder and turn around to face the wall, sliding my panties down between my knees.

"Fuck me like a whore."

Where did *that* come from? No idea. He goes limp instantly, soft like a makeup sponge, getting absolutely nowhere, and all I can feel is my ass freezing. We give up and walk back to the apartment in awkward silence.

Too drunk to take my clothes off, I pass out spread-eagled on the bed. My mouth smells like ass, and I'm getting nauseous. The floor in the hallway cracks, and my bedroom door whines.

"Can I come in?"

"Uh-huh."

Raphael starts to take my clothes off and gently kisses every part of my body. He goes down on me so passionately that I start giggling nervously.

"Fuck …! You're … fucking … good …"

Energized, I slip my mouth around his cock until he comes on my sheets. Lasted all of forty-five seconds. Exhausted down to our bones, we ditch the mess in my bed for his room.

* * *

I go through customs with a faraway look in my eyes. Can the X-ray scanner see the dried cum on my wrist?

Tania greets me in the new VIP lounge for Air Something. Everything is wrapped in leather, shiny, clinks like marble. She finds us a spot between the gate screens and the toilets. I have to wash my hands.

I spread out my makeup brushes at a snail's pace while Tania explains her vision for the photo shoot while handling emails and checking her already perfect hair.

"We're trying to capture youth, glamour — we want it to be sexy without being trashy. The models are the winning couple of a new reality TV dating show. You seen it? It's fucking lame. We want her to look natural but perfect — 'I just got back from a five-star yoga retreat in Bali' — you know? And him. We want to see his muscles and tattoos. The market loves that, very millennial, whatever. Shandy has the costumes if you need inspiration. By the way, I increased your fee. You definitely won't be wasting your time. My god, this skirt makes me look so fat."

By some miracle, I manage to do Shandy's contouring without throwing up in her lap. I dig my fingers into my palm to keep myself from trembling while I finish her makeup and turn her into a star. She doesn't need to know that I've used the same brush on a hundred dead people with faces oddly more alive than hers.

Barbie and Ken pose on a featureless yellow leather sofa, fake champagne in their hands and wind in their hair. Tania joins me in the corner, where I discreetly watch my work in action, and takes her pumps off with a grumble. My head instinctively falls to her shoulder.

"At the club, yesterday, we met a real hottie. I've never seen anything like her, Philly. Long black hair, remastered tits, perfect mouth … So, I spot her, I offer her a drink, and we start talking at the bar … Smart, funny, eloquent. I introduce her to Daniel, and he's instantly hard as hell. She finds him attractive, but I'm obviously the one she wants. She likes women better than men … Anyway, we fucked in the goth room. It was lots of fun. We traded phone numbers. I think we'll see each other again. Hey, you listening to me?"

"Yeah, sorry. I'm trashed. Only slept an hour."

"Who'd you sleep with?"

"No one."

"Wait, hold on … with Raphael?"

"No …"

"Hah. I knew it. I told you it would happen."

"We didn't have sex, Tan. We just … had really good foreplay, okay?"

"Oh my god, tell me more."

"It was a one-time thing, that's it. We were drunk."

You swear it'll never happen again, blah blah blah, but I know you, Philly. Your eyes are shiny, and it has nothing to do with how tired you are. You're finally falling for something real.

* * *

Raphael is rewatching the festival's official selection for the thousandth time. Tomorrow is Nitrate's opening night. But tonight, his legs are shaking under his big quilt.

Thirteen hundred hours of screen time just to choose the twenty experimental films for the festival's third edition. I kept him company throughout the whole process with a level of interest that surprised me. It was nice to see people moving, talking, breathing, for a change. Raphael took note of all my thoughts, my design comments. We talk endlessly about narrative arcs and artistic choices. When Marie-Christine joins us in the living room, there isn't enough space on the sofa.

Raphael can't stay still — he has anxiety attack written all over his face.

"My parents are coming down from the Saguenay. What if it's all shit?"

"Your mom is your biggest fan. She'll love it, for sure."

"Right. The tickets, they're barely selling. What if people don't show up? The guys are counting on me, the sponsors are counting on me …"

"Raph! Nitrate is doing great. People love it. Don't worry, it'll be fine."

The guy who's supposed to be an unflappable force is curled up like a grub worm on the floor. If Raph is freaked, the rest of us should find a bridge to jump off. Okay. Crisis mode. Time to soothe his male ego.

Cocks are all the same, but his is really sweet. I'm disarmed by how sensitive it is, how his body responds to mine, how he puts his hands on my body, how his beard feels on my skin. How long has it been since I've had sex without playing any games?

"Sap-filled vines began to unfurl from between the Woman's ribs. Not knowing why it felt so drawn to this corpse, the Creature set about tearing apart every growth and bud that had sprouted from its dead wife's skeleton. Yet, for each root torn out, two more grew in its place. The Kingdom of Shadows had grown fertile despite the land's inherent hostility."

Shit. I'm really in trouble.

We lie naked in his bed when Marie-Christine comes back home.

"Raph! I have a surprise for you. Raph?"

She nearly drops the champagne bottle when she finds us half naked in his bed.

"What's going on?"

He gratefully thanks her for the gift and promptly runs to the kitchen to get champagne flutes. Marie-Christine stares at me with poorly concealed loathing. My shirt is inside out.

"Something wrong?"

"No. No, but I'm warning you, Philomena, I'm not going to let you hurt him."

"C'mon, relax …"

"Raph is a good guy. He deserves someone who'll treat him right."

"Don't worry, Marie. I know."

"The Creature, refusing to see such defiant life in his perfect wasteland, shuttered the windows, barred up the doors, and filled in even the tiniest cracks in its castle walls, drowning out the undying beauty threatening his eternal darkness."

21

The snow is melting in the yard. The sun got lost on the way back from the Caribbean. Spring is being a tease, showing up this early; everybody knows a storm is just around the corner. I have to take advantage of my free time to work on "In Your Human Hands," but I've lost my momentum. The corpses of old cigarettes stud the muddy ground. I've started smoking again, like a fucking idiot. Marie-Christine opens the gate, arms full of groceries.

"Ugh. That stinks."

She's just begging me to spit in her face. Raphael follows after her with a huge bag of kitty litter, happy as ever. Nitrate was a huge hit again this year. He's even thinking of taking it international.

"Want to hang out with us in the kitchen, Philly? We're going to make a big batch of spaghetti sauce and a seafood pie from scratch."

"No, thanks."

"Everything okay?"

"Yeah."

"Why are you acting weird?"

"I'm not acting weird, Raph. I just want to relax. Alone."

I've been pulling back since Marie-Christine freaked out at me. The bitch might just be right. Even I know that I'm a monster, and all I'm going to do is hurt her precious Raph. She's obviously in love with him. They'd be perfect together.

"Have you decided if you'll come to Look? I've booked a room at the Chicoutimi Hotel, if you want to."

"Can't. I'm on call at the funeral home."

"You can't get someone to replace you?"

"No, Raphael, I can't. I'm easy to replace in a lot of other ways but not at work."

"I didn't mean to insult you."

"I know."

"I just thought that …"

"That because they're dead, they've got nothing better to do than wait around for me? Well, no. That's not how it works. They may not be as *successful* as you are, but they still don't deserve to rot just to make you feel better. Okay?"

"All right. I got it."

"Why don't you invite Marie-Christine instead? She'd cream her little panties."

"What's wrong?"

"Nothing."

"It feels like something's changed over the past few weeks, Philly."

"Yeah, well, it's just a feeling. I'm doing great, and I'd really like for you to invite Marie-Christine to go with you. It'd do me some good to have the apartment to myself.

"Do you … regret that we made love?"

"First of all, we fucked. We didn't make love. Second of all, sure, it was fun, but it didn't mean anything. You're my roommate."

He puts the kitty litter on the ground with a grunt.

"Damn, Philly."

"What?"

"You're more than just a roommate to me! You're my friend, and I really care about you."

"Yeah, well. Me, too …"

"No, obviously not. But you know me, I just see love in every face I see."

"Raph."

"All right. We'll do it your way. No muss, no fuss. If you want to fuck, just let me know."

* * *

One thirty in the morning and I'm downing shots of lime-flavoured vodka with reckless abandon. Tania describes Sexy-Toy Sonia's every bodily detail with each gulp.

"Eating pussy is just so hard. I feel like a retard. Cheers."

The loud music makes my ears flair; Tania has to yell every word.

"She's a squirter, too. Did you know that all of us can squirt? I read it on a blog. You just need to work out your pelvic muscles. I'm almost there."

"Oh, really?"

"But I'm worried."

"*You're* worried?"

"Sometimes … I worry that Daniel thinks she's prettier than I am. She's so skinny, Philly."

"Don't worry, Tan. You're the queen. She's just a toy. Cheers."

A naked guy next to me and a puddle of puke at the foot of the bed. Fuck. The apartment looks like a tornado blew through it, and the roommates are coming back soon … Cold shower doesn't straighten me out. I'm getting too old for this shit. I shake the nameless guy awake with my foot. He finally opens his eyes. His face is covered with sheet marks. We do the morning-after routine.

"I don't mean to rush you, but do you think you could leave now? I'm going to breakfast with my mom."

* * *

Her face is red and her nose is leaking. She hasn't even done her hair. I rub her back on autopilot, too distracted trying to keep the eggs benedict and bile down. My mom's heart is broken. Raymond cheated on her with a younger, blonder woman. She always suspected it, but when she caught him screwing his mistress she had to believe it.

"He swears that the sex means nothing, that I'm the love of his life, that it just happened one time … He really thinks I'm an idiot. I can't believe it. I'm all alone, Philomena. He's even threatening to take Yappy away if I don't come back home. What am I going to do?"

She should have spent more time building herself up instead of latching on to some guy, but you can't say that to your own mom.

"You could come live at my place for a while."

"Really?"

"Uh-huh."

"Oh, baby, oh, honey, that's so nice of you. What should we do about Yappy?"

The door to the big house on the mountainside opens to show Raymond, acting devastated.

"I never meant to hurt your mom, Philomena."

"I know. You always treated her so well. I'm here to get the dog. Move."

"If she wants it, she can come and get it. Either way, she can't live alone. She doesn't know how to take care of herself. I'm the one who pays for everything. How does she think she'll get by without my credit card?"

"How do you think *you'll* get by with broken *legs*?"

Raphael gets out of the car with a baseball bat in his hands. He's wearing dark Ray-Bans to look dangerous. Raymond may be tall, but he's got hamster balls. He very politely lets me leave with Yappy.

"Your mom's addicted to being in love. She's so needy — she'll suck the life out of you."

"Better my life than your wrinkly pecker, eh, Ray?"

"Don't you dare talk to me like that. I met her when she was at rock bottom. I'm the reason why her life is going so well right now. I will *not let* her humiliate me. You tell her that if she doesn't come back home, I will bring her back home. Is that understood?"

"Listen up, Jack. If you go anywhere near her, I swear to you that I will personally paint a dick on your face in the basement of Memorium. Is *that* understood?"

Yappy and I are trembling as we drive away in the beat-up Tercel. Raphael holds my hand, comforts me. His gangster getup cracks me up.

In the Orange Julep parking lot, mouth full of burger, he starts to open up. He slept with Marie-Christine after the Look Festival closing party. Of course. I start to choke on my cheeseburger.

"I'm … I'm happy for you. She's always wanted to be with you."

"Yeah, but I don't feel fireworks, you know?"

"What do you mean?"

"It was … subdued."

"Good for you. Subdued is just what you need, Raph."

"I think that Marie-Christine is in love with me."

"Yeah. Has been for a long time."

"It doesn't make any sense."

"What?"

"The girl who wants to be with me … isn't the one I want. I want to be with the girl who doesn't care about me."

"Did she actually say that she doesn't care about you?"

"I don't know … do you care about me?"

"I can't get attached, Raph. I can't do it anymore."

"I can wait. Take all the time you need."

"Don't say that. I'm not the right girl for you. I'm no good — for anyone."

"Trapped in the dark, the flowers growing out of the Woman's corpse begin to wither. Soon, there will be nothing but thorns left among the bones."

Mom is curled in a ball on my bed, her little dog clasped to her chest.

"I never could have made it without you."

"Nah, Mom. Just rest."

"You know what gave me the strength to get out of there?"

"What?"

"Your father's letter. I hadn't read it, couldn't bring myself to. But a few months ago, when I asked Ray if he was seeing other women and he lied straight to my face, then called me crazy, I opened the letter. It made me realize how much … how much I miss being in love, Philly. Really, simply … honestly in love. I ruined everything with your dad. I ruined it by wanting pretty, expensive things … I ruined it. And I can never get it back. I ruined my life …"

I take my mom in my arms and rock her, telling her that everything happens for a reason and that we always learn from our mistakes.

I wish.

My mom slowly comes back to life. Marie-Christine heals her soul with her fucking aromatherapy. I hate it. Mom, with Yappy and Tigger — the new gay couple of 2817 rue Hochelaga — sleep in my bed, and I've moved into Raphael's. It smells like man and springtime. I don't dream anymore; I fantasize. At first, I would watch him sleep on the couch before going to work. There was something beautiful about his body in the early morning light. But now the living room is empty, and Marie-Christine's door is always locked. I hate them, too.

I work like crazy, drink too much, and drive myself dizzy with stupid dating apps. I will not think about him.

But when I get back from work to find him cooking with my mom, or playing Scrabble, or working on his media platform while listening to Latin music, I just die. Just like dead trees shattered by the freezing winter, I crack. And I hate myself.

"That boy is just so nice, honey. He'd be a great boyfriend. I can tell."

"Then ask him out, Mom. Marie-Christine might not be your friend anymore but …"

"Do you know who he reminds me of?"

"No, who?"

"Your father."

Her words come as such a surprise that I don't even realize the tears have started pouring down my face until I notice how wet my cheeks have become. She holds me against her; I don't want her to touch me. I'm fine.

"It's all right to cry, honey. That's what mourning is."

"I'm not crying."

"Your eyes are red, Philly."

"It's … because of … Tigger."

"Yeah, must be. You're not even allergic to cats."

"You told me I was."

"So you would stop bothering me. Cats leave hair all over the place. They're unhealthy. Did you know that Yappy's fur isn't hair, that it's actually wool? It's a *lot* better."

Fuck me, Mom.

I manage to convince her to start looking for a job. She needs to become independent.

"I don't have any skills. No one's going to hire me. I'm too old."

"C'mon, Mom. You have to believe in yourself."

"It's hard when you're my age, when you've lost everything. I don't have anything left without Raymond."

"A little freedom and self-respect have been good for you, don't you think?"

"I don't even know where to start, Philomena."

"What do you like? What are your interests?"

"Nothing."

"Mom."

"Okay. Okay. I like … fashion?"

"That's perfect."

"Really?"

"We're going downtown."

"To Montreal?"

"Uh, yeah?"

"In the metro?"

"That a problem?"

"No, no."

Now that she's officially a luxury lingerie salesperson and nearly over her fear of the metro, Mom drinks up her new freedom and talks enthusiastically about being at work. Looking for an apartment comes as her own idea. She instantly falls in love with a little one-bedroom with a communal garden and a roof-top balcony. The owner wasn't too happy with the dog, but since Yappy is the size of a rat he got past it. My mom signs her first lease at fifty, happy as a kid at Christmas.

22

Drunk and alone at seven o'clock. Tigger, the cat, is the only one to stay and give me hugs. He misses his furry boyfriend. I feel for him. I'd like to have someone to rub my face on, too. Only there's no one left in the apartment, just the sound of traffic. Daniel is filming his short in Banff, Tania followed after him; Raphael and Marie-Christine are at hot yoga. Their relationship is coming together nicely. They snuggle on the couch more often, giggle together about everything; I'm at peak aggravation. I have to do something with myself. I could get my manuscript out and work on some panels. I've beaten the Woman's body so badly that she just looks like a wound. I've always thought that broken bodies are strangely beautiful. I'll have to work on the shadowing, play with the volumes, and revise the manuscript ... Fuck, I wish I were in a coma.

Rue Sainte-Catherine is full of sparkling lights, and the wet air freezes me down to my bones. I pop in to Taverne Midway to warm up with a Glenlivet. I hate whisky. Why do I keep drinking it? I need a personality of my own. People are having a birthday party in the back. Sebastien Strasbourg peels off from the pack of jackals to order some shots at the bar. There are no coincidences.

"Philomena? Philly, it's been forever! You look great."

After a quick kiss on the cheek, Seb whispers in my ear that he has "fucking amazing powder, if you want ..." I instantly perk up and follow him into the bathrooms. Quick key bump, easy as pie. I join the bunch of monkeys, play foosball, down shot after shot, re-up my high, French-kiss the birthday boy, run away before he asks for a happy ending. Dizzy, puke climbing up my throat. "WHERE ARE THE FUCKING CABS?" I throw up in the entrance of the corner store. A bunch of girls in skirts that don't even cover their asses laugh in my face. Fuck off, sluts. I feel the touch of a warm hand on my back.

"I bought a bottle of water. You wanna sit? Here, put my coat on."

Fuck, I'm going to pass out. I spit a mouthful of bile and try to keep the next one down; Sebastien keeps me from falling over.

Make it stop.

* * *

My eyes open in a panic. What time is it? There's dried vomit on my blue jacket, and two black smears of mascara under my eyes. I get out of bed fucked to high hell. I need to order some poutine. The roommates are eating across from each other in awkward silence. Raphael asks me if I slept well.

"Uh … yeah. Were you the one …"

Marie-Christine glares at me with her fucking bitch face.

"Who do you think paid for your cab, got you into bed, helped you put your pyjamas on? Cleaned your puke off the floor, *twice*? Rubbed your back for hours because it was the only thing that made you feel better? Him. He did all that. For you. Raph did all of that for *you*. Could you be at least a *little* grateful?"

My head is buzzing. She can obviously see my face fall in discomfort. Raphael begs her to quiet down.

"No, I won't calm down. If she wants to act like a child, I'm going to treat her like a child. Your behaviour is disgusting. It isn't our job to clean up the apartment every time you get fucking trashed."

"What's your problem this morning?"

"It isn't morning, anymore. It's six o'clock. Your lifestyle is fucking everything up, Philomena."

"Mind your own fucking business."

"Girls, not so loud."

"I'm going to mind my own business when Raph doesn't have to spend his nights making sure you don't choke on your own vomit."

"That's your problem! You're jealous."

"Fuck you."

"That's it, Marie, you're jealous! He takes care of me, cuddles with me, touches me. That's what's killing you, right?"

"You're fucking sick."

"He doesn't love you as much as me."

"Eat shit, Philomena."

"You eat shit."

"Girls, that's *enough*."

My turn to be broken-hearted and need a place to stay. She feeds me vegetable soup and Tylenol.

"Aren't you sick a lot these days, honey? You should go see a doctor."

"I'm just tired, Mom."

"It's probably your thyroid."

"Yeah. Probably. What's new with you?"

Mom takes me through the new spring collection in detail.

"I'm wearing Sweet Passion right now. The top is perfect, really makes my boobs super perky. With a little cleavage, I'm going to slay."

She leaves to have birthday supper with a co-worker. Alone with *Titanic*, I wake up to Kate kissing Leonardo's fingertips. "Put your hands on me, Jack." Hands, love, death: I can't get away from them. I need to smarten up and work on my book. What am I waiting for? To become a fucking loser while everyone around me is happy? Yappy won't stop whining, so I get my sad, fat, alcoholic ass off the couch and take a walk down Mont-Royal. A text from Sebastien asks me how my hangover is going. "Bad. I got into a fight with my roommate and I'm starving." He suggests that we smoke a joint and get some pizza. Better than nothing.

At Fameux deli, we chow down like pigs at a trough. Yappy sleeps in the booth, hidden under my dad's sweater. I'm cold. Sebastien looks pretty fucked up, too.

"I'm barely getting any auditions. Things are dead right now. I make webisodes with my boys, but we don't make any money. Mind if I take a fry?"

"Uh-huh. Didn't you write poetry?"

"Yeah. I read stuff at Belmont on Sunday nights. You should come."

"Maybe."

"How about you?"

"What?"

"You working on something?"

"Uh … I'm writing a graphic novel."

"That's great. Can't wait to read it."

"Yeah … I don't know. I'm kind of too shy to send it to anyone … there are so many good ones out there."

"Yeah? So? There is only one Philly Flynn."

The waiter brings us our bills. Sebastien "forgot" his wallet, so I cover him. He offers to walk me back home. No. We will definitely not go back to my mom's place to hang out. Not a chance.

"Come to Belmont tomorrow. I always love seeing you."

He goes to kiss my cheek, but his warm lips end up at the corner of my mouth. A wink and he dives into La Rockette, a real pickup bar. How is he going to pay for his drinks? That's the best part about being an actor: stardom is its own currency. I collapse onto the sofa, feet swollen from walking too much. I'm miserable because I'm going to have to move out. Sebastien texts me to say that I'm a hundred times prettier than I was last year.

Raphael digs his tongue into all my orifices; I want to come, but I can't get a sound out. Sheets of rain fall into the tiny, freezing room. I want to run, fight him off, but Raphael is too strong. His face fades away. He morphs into an enormous snake, fangs gleaming in the moonlight. He's going to tear my throat out, but Dad chops his head off. Dad is there, standing in front of me. He smells like spaghetti. Mrs. Jorish cries in my arms. Dad flies off, flapping giant duck wings.

Half asleep, I scramble for a piece of paper, anything.

"After years of darkness and loneliness, a beam of light breaks into the chamber where the Woman's body lies covered in a blanket of withered flowers. When the beam falls on the corpse, the Creature, alone in his throne room, begins to cry, tears that rip themselves from some forgotten organ. Its memory suddenly comes back, freed from the pact he made with the Serpent — broken by an even more powerful force.

A single forget-me-not begins to grow in the Woman's skeletal hand. *I will never forget you.*"

And then, it's right there on the page. The end. I'm going to do it for him. For Dad. Before going to get Tania at the airport, I transcribe the ending that just came to me onto the computer, print copies of the best panels, and send the manuscript to the publishing houses that look like the best fit. I hold the thick envelopes to my chest before sliding them into the mailbox.

The ancient Tercel is stuck in a massive traffic jam. Tania punctuates every word by punching her suitcase.

"A fucking break! He wants us to take a break! What does that even mean? Everyone know that a break is just a breakup in disguise. Love is fucking shit, and I never should have trusted that asshole. Can you believe that I *didn't* cheat on him last summer?"

"It'll be all right, Tan."

Why didn't you tell me that having a threesome with another girl was a terrible idea? Why didn't you argue with me? Convince me? Do I scare people off? Is that it? No. It won't be all right, Philly. Nothing'll be all right. Why does everything have to go to shit?

I take the first available exit and speed all the way to the McDonald's. Hearts pour out of Tania's eyes. Medium fries, ketchup, ten McNuggets, cheeseburger, Coke, sweet and sour sauce, McChicken, large fries, Sprite, no, Coke, no, Sprite, ketchup, vinegar, and an Oreo McFlurry. My car smells like a dump.

"It isn't the fact that they're fucking that bothers me, it's that they're having a relationship behind my back, you know? I mean … he's replacing me, Philly. He'd rather text a girl with fake tits than have a real conversation with the girlfriend who came all the way to Banff to fucking surprise him. Fuck. I really need a drink."

Belmont is packed with young artists, each one a bigger hipster than the last. At a table in the back, I pretend to like gin and tonics while Tania pounds back glasses of Sex on the Beach.

"Fuck my shitty job, fuck Daniel, and fuck my fat fucking thighs. Let's do some shots."

Like a magnet drawn to chaos, Sebastien shows up with a bottle of Goldschläger. I hate cinnamon. Tania downs my glass while Sebastien makes googly eyes at me.

"I'm not here to see you, Seb. I'm here to make my friend feel better."

"Don't be cranky, Philly. I'm just happy to see you, that's all."

Tania undoes her blouse's top button and orders her millionth drink.

"Chill out, Tan. You aren't single, yet. It's just a break."

"He can shove his break right up his ass. It's not like we're married … Oh my god, Philly. I have to tell you something …"

"What?"

"Guess who I had to have supper with the other day?"

Jeffrey. She must have seen Jeff with his new girlfriend, insanely happy, sexier than ever. Jeff and Angelica, couple of the year. Or maybe they aren't together anymore? Maybe I was right and it was just a rebound, and he got sick of Saint Angelica. Maybe he told Tania how much better it was when we were together? My heart is vibrating. I can't breathe.

"So? How was it?"

"Fine."

"Just fine?"

"Having a little money trouble, actually …"

"Why? Didn't their fucking food truck work out?"

"No. No, it's working. But … big expenses on the way …"

"What?"

"They're engaged."

Goddamn fucking piece of motherfucking shit. I swallow every drop of alcohol left on the table, and I wave until the waiter sees that I need a fresh drink. Now.

"I didn't know if I should tell you."

I knew that I absolutely had *to be the one to tell you. So you don't find out all alone on a bad night when you break down and stalk his Facebook page. You have to rip this Band-Aid off, once and for all, so you can finally heal. I'm sorry to be the one to hurt you, but it's better than accidentally stabbing yourself in the heart. Right?*

"I can't believe it, Tania! It's just been a year … That was fast, wasn't it?"

"Yeah …"

"Jeff's getting married? He's going to be her husband. Angelica's husband. Fuck."

"Yeah."

"What is she? Pregnant? She have cancer?"

"No. I think they're in love."

Son of a motherfucking piece of goddamn shit.

"I didn't mean to get you all fucked up."

"I'm okay."

"You sure?"

"Uh-huh, when is it?"

"They haven't picked a date yet."

"They're going to live out there?"

"Yup. Angelica's parents live close to Lake Louise … Jeff loves skiing, they kite-board in the summer …"

"Yuck."

"I know."

My heart is buried in a block of cement, and cramps are twisting up my guts. The familiar nauseous feeling wraps around my throat and temples.

Sebastien is naked on top of me, eyes wide, mouth slack. He doesn't get it.

"Hit me. I want you to hit me."

"You want me to hit you …"

"I'm telling you to do it, Seb. If you're too big a pussy, say so, and I'll get out of here."

"You want me to hit you in the face?"

"My face, my tits, spank my ass off. Yeah, it's what I want."

"I … can't."

"The fuck, Strasbourg."

The first slap puts some blood back in my cheek. The second, harder, more confident, almost splits my lip. His hands reach clumsily around my neck, but he actually manages to choke me. He lets me breathe at the last second, flips me over, and fucks me from behind like he's got a gun to his head.

After a few minutes, he takes off the empty condom with a sad look.

"Seriously, Philly. You're a lot of fun, but if that's what gets you off, I think you've got the wrong guy."

I just wanted to get the knot of pain and bitterness out of my throat. I just wanted to forget I had ever laid eyes on Jeffrey Hudon.

I move what little I own into a shitty hotel room. Raphael tries to convince me to stay in the apartment, but there's no way I can. The more I think about it, Marie-Christine might have actually been right. She *should* make him happy. I'm all fucked up, anyway.

23

Latin Quarter, Summer 2018

I love the Star Hotel. It's cheap and dirty. The prostitutes bring their johns here. Right where I belong. I'm a big spender; I rent by the week. Like a twenty-year-old, but worse. Tania is out of the country. Gone to Colombia with Daniel. It isn't the relationship that ended, it was their lease. They're trying to mix things up, change things. I knew I'd lose her.

All my cadavers end up looking sad. I can't recognize the colours on my makeup palette. Sometimes I want to take my gas mask off, breathe those toxic fumes deep, and just fade away. Everything would be so quiet, so simple on the slab. But no. I keep working and keep breathing.

For the entire month of May, not a day goes by without my body being pierced by a new penis. The cleaning lady looks at me with horror. Fuck off, old cow. Raphael texts me all the time, even though my answers are no more than three letters long. I'm going to have to change my number if this keeps up.

To celebrate Saint-Jean-Baptiste Day, I have a gangbang with some douchebags from the South Shore. I know just one of the seven of them. Used to be a friend of Louis's once upon a time. His dick is tiny. Poor guy.

But I don't discriminate. I celebrate Canada Day, too. Three sleepless days go by, ground raw by the ecstasy, fucking a morbidly obese guy from Saskatchewan.

The Star Hotel is like the Twilight Zone — things disappear and nothing makes sense. The tall anxious guy in 102 asks how much I charge. I don't bat an eye and let him fuck me in the ass for free. I'm no whore, c'mon. He gives me his pack of smokes. Good tipper.

I'm not pushing my limits, yet.

Noon in a heatwave. July chases the sweat down my spine. I've spent all morning working on a dead lady, and all I want to do is cry. I get out of my car with a half-rolled joint. I'm going to call ... what's his name? Matthew? Matias? Fucked if I know ... He works nights, too. Even though he fucks like a hopped-up chihuahua, his dick is big enough that I don't even mind. The joint slips out of my hands. Shit, it better not get fucked up.

Raphael catches it in midair before it falls into a manhole. If it's a small world, what does that say about Montreal?

"Hey, Philly."

"Hey."

"What's going on?"

"I'm going to work."

"I just finished work. We're on two different planets, aren't we?"

He looks fresh and clean in his T-shirt. Not sweating at all. His shoulders look bigger. Tall, strong, welcoming. My exact opposite.

"It's nice to see you. I miss you."

"You want a puff?"

"No, thanks. I'm conducting a seminar at UQAM."

"Oh, wow, dude. That's great. Congrats."

"Are you okay?"

"Top of the world."

"Okay. I'm here for you, if you need anything."

Fuck you. I don't need your help. I've never been happier! Purple Kush is the air I breathe.

"Say hi to your girlfriend for me."

"Marie-Christine and I aren't together anymore."

"What the fuck are you two waiting for? Me to fucking die?"

"What are you talking about?"

"I don't know. I'm a bitch."

"That's a lie. You know how amazing and talented I think you are."

I don't know if it's him or the weed, but I laugh until I get a face cramp.

"Talented? Don't make me laugh. I just got my first rejection letter for my graphic novel. You think that's talent?"

"I'm sorry …"

"Don't be sorry. I'm just a fucking idiot. I should never have sent it."

He offers to buy me a coffee. We could talk, maybe even cry together while holding hands. He just wants me to get better.

"No, thanks. I don't have time for a coffee. There's a dude coming by for a fuck. Have a nice day, Raphael."

Early August. I'm tired of meeting the same losers in the same lame bars. Tired of the fucking pain that won't let me go. I need some sense knocked into me. *Dom looking to play power games with an obedient sub.* Thank god for Craigslist. Patrick Steben, thirtysomething, bleached teeth, executive at a big company, has been domming for five years and is just what I'm looking for. We message each other a little through the website. He asks me what I'm looking for.

"I just want you to hurt me."

"What else?"

"I'm a slut, Patrick. I want you to violate me."

He sets a time for us to meet so we can see if we're a good fit. My room smells like cigarette smoke and spilled beer.

"My subs don't smoke. You're going to quit."

Yes, sir. But you had better beat me stupid.

"Lie down on the bed, on your stomach."

He flips my skirt onto my lower back and tugs my panties down to my knees. His leather belt strikes my soft white skin.

"Fuck!"

Tears start to pool in my eyes … Can't … catch my breath. Fuck. He pauses for a few seconds, then hits me again.

And, like that, we click.

24

Blainville, August 2018

My Tercel crosses the North Shore, and I park in front of a big house in the suburbs, a lame greystone castle.

I become his personal slave the moment I open the door. Today, Patrick ties me up, whips me, spits on me. I moan as a riding crop slaps my skin.

"You're just a little slut, desperate for attention. Do you actually think that anyone could ever fucking love you?"

I don't even know who's speaking. The emptiness inside me goes from my centre all the way out to my skin. He bites my inner thighs so hard that they bleed. My hands are tied behind my back. The louder I yell, the harder he bites.

"Who owns you?"

"You do."

"What's my name?"

"Jeff. Jeffrey Hudon."

"Look at me when I hit you."

I ram his cock to the back of my throat, like I'm trying to knock my hair off. I have drool all over my chest. This must be hitting bottom. This must be it.

Patrick never gets off inside me. He pulls his dick out of my throat and ties a collar around my neck. He tugs on the leash: the skin on my neck rubs against the leather, and I automatically get on all fours.

Who's a good bitch, now? My knees are raw from rug burn. His hand grabs my jaw so hard that it pops.

"Tilt your hips forward."

He eats me out like a starving man. Juice is running from my pussy down to my knees. Does Angelica let Jeffrey fuck her like this?

Tears quietly slide down my cheeks while he pisses on me.

Happy birthday, you fucking slut.

The air smells delicious, the lights are low, and a light opera plays as we eat. Patrick has made us two perfect dragon bowls, and I've garnished them with edible flowers. Goddamn flowers! I finish my second glass of wine before my first mouthful of jasmine fucking rice. Patrick goes on about Wagner, who literally changed the way he sees art, while wolfing down his supper. My jaw hurts too much to chew, and I'm happy to open a second bottle of wine. He recommends a special vintage from the lovely Italian countryside. Like I give a fuck.

"One of my import-export clients owns an amazing villa in the south of Naples; I'll be spending a few weeks, there. Then we'll visit vineyards in his convertible."

"You're leaving?"

"About three months."

"You're kidding me."

"Not at all."

"You can't go, Pat."

"You're giving me orders, now?"

"No, but … I still need … Who am I going to …?"

"You'll find someone else, Philomena."

"Fuck, Patrick. I was doing so well, I was just getting nice and numb. You can't do this to me."

"I can do whatever I please."

I can hardly stand up by the end of my birthday. Twenty-eight and all alone, puke all over my Tercel. If my father saw me, he'd die all fucking over again.

Back in my room at the Star, I tie a rope around the bar holding up my shower curtain. I'm on my way, Daddy. I'll be there soon. Just give me the strength to let go. Send me a sign. My feet slip off the edge of the bathtub, and my back hits the bottom of the tub. The bar hits me in the face a second later. A shower of cheap tile sprinkles down on me.

I wanted to kill myself. All I did was break my nose.

The only reason they don't put me under observation is because I lie my ass off.

"I was trying to do a chin-up, but the bar wasn't strong enough."

The nurse doesn't ask any questions, just patches me up and asks if someone's coming to get me. Nope. No one. She tells me it's a bad idea to be alone, because I might have a concussion.

I suffer silently, naked in the bathtub. Broken. Marie-Christine yells at him in the hallway. Their voices are muddy, but I get the point. She hates that he keeps saving me, always and forever. He tells her that's what you do for someone you love.

He lends me his Nitrate sweater, makes me tea, food. I don't have the strength to chew a grape; I'm just a dry leaf waiting to get crushed.

"What's happening to you, Philly? Is something wrong?"

"Yes."

"What's wrong?"

"Me."

I find Mrs. Jorish's old yellow housecoat. It got lost in the back of a closet, with my dignity. I fall asleep on Raphael's bed, the same as before, except now it smells like autumn. He's a warm, safe spoon behind me. Maybe when I wake up, this'll all just be a dream?

No. The morning rises as real as everything else that's been happening. I have to leave before I drag him down, too.

"You're leaving?"

"I don't want to bother you ... I don't think that Marie-Christine ..."

"Marie's gone."

"Oh. Okay."

"It's okay if you don't want to talk. I just want to have breakfast with my friend. I miss you, Philly."

The walls are starting to suffocate me, so we walk down to the river. The air feels warm, but I shiver uncontrollably, chilled to my core. We watch the St. Lawrence roll by from a bench on the bank. Raphael takes my hand and kisses my fingertips with heartbreaking tenderness.

And I'm not so cold anymore.

25

September's first cool days barely reach me where I lie wrapped in Raphael's warmth. Even the cadavers at Memorium look happier; my colour palette has got warmer. I've started eating, laughing, swimming again. But one person's happiness always ends up pissing someone else off.

Marie-Christine left her keys on the kitchen table with a letter dripping with hate. She took Tigger with her. It's my turn to make Raphael feel better. I finally use some of my vacation days and use the time to take a secret dream out of hiding, something that will make both of us feel good.

When I was with Martin, I fantasized about it. When I was with Jeff, it just seemed too banal. I've wanted to go apple picking with a guy since I was ten years old. It's cheesy, but it's what I want. When Tania and I fantasized inside our living room fort about our grown-up lives, I wanted a tall guy with smooth cheeks who would lift me up while I plucked perfectly rosy apples from their branches. Tania wanted to be a wild horse trainer and to have lovers in every country to take care of the houses everywhere she wanted to live.

I miss my best friend. But she doesn't feel so far away. Last week she sent me a picture of her with *abuelita* Yoselin, Daniel's long-lost grandma. They were riding donkeys, with the Andes behind them. Free.

We made it, Tan. Not the way we thought we would, but we had no way of knowing that the reality would be even better than the dream.

Raphael and I pick apples. Real apples from real trees, with a ladder, a basket, and all. Kids everywhere and McIntoshes covered in caramel. I love it. I can hear Tania calling us lame in the back of my mind.

We nibble on cheese curds while listening to the *Moulin Rouge!* soundtrack on the drive back. Fresh cheese curds! Since when do I have such great ideas?

We run low on gas, and we make out against the gas pump; people honk impatiently. They're just jealous. A vanilla sky spreads out overhead, pink and blue. The sun is setting and I'm finally starting to feel alive.

"Do you want to see something really special?"

We head deeper into the woods to my private hideaway. We rake the leaves and make love in the big fluffy piles. Finally,

Halloween smells like something other than vomit. I introduce Raphael to the lake where my dad drifts with the current. We make an enormous bonfire, tell each other our darkest secrets and craziest dreams, laugh like I haven't laughed in years. We do a slow dance between the fridge and the toilet. Such an amazing dance. Wind up snuggling on a mattress on the floor in front of the TV, where the loveseat used to be, captivated by *Diamonds Are Forever*.

I do a preliminary poster sketch for next year's Nitrate Festival. Raphael loves it. We bounce ideas off each other, I work on my book proposal, he sings in the kitchen. It's all so amazing that I want to tell him I'm falling in love with him. And, for the first time in my life, I fall, but I only fall into his arms, sweetly, beautifully.

"What are you thinking about?"

"What colour bow tie you could wear this year."

His mouth meets mine in midair; there's sauce all over my neck. Our kisses taste like tacos. Suddenly I'm Frida, and Raphael is my most amazing canvas.

October is right around the corner. We greet it snuggling next to the wood-burning stove.

"I feel so much better in the country. The city drives me crazy, I guess."

"I feel the same way. I need space, too. And I'd rather not raise my kids next to noisy busy streets."

"You want kids?"

"Yeah. Maybe not as many as my parents, though. I'd start with just the one. How about you?"

I spend the rest of my vacation capturing the autumn colours, making love all over the cottage, burying old memories with better ones. We close the cottage for the winter and go back to the city, a little sad we have to leave. But my head on Raphael's shoulder makes it better.

Shattered sidewalks and endless orange cones are everywhere in Hochelaga. Alley cats stalk streets that smell like wet garbage. Welcome home. The apartment looks like it's lost weight, gotten smaller, darker. I find Tigger's furballs hidden in lonely corners. The place smells empty. Our homecoming hits me like a ton of bricks. Raphael's smile is the only thing that brightens up this shitty town.

Our phones ding nonstop; email tumbles out like crazy: back in civilization and its Wi-Fi embrace.

> Hello, Ms. Flynn. I was unable to contact you by phone, so please forgive me for contacting you by email. Our selection committee is pleased to inform you that your manuscript has been unanimously selected, and we would be thrilled to publish your first book. We hope to meet you in person so that we may begin the publishing process.
>
> Cécile Claude, Editor, Plume Publishing.

I scream with joy until I fall asleep. Every day turns into a holiday in Raphael's proud ginger embrace, as again and again we sing "Come What May."

26

The rain pelts down on Gaspésie unforgivingly. Show me the way, Daddy.

There's nothing better than being stuck in a car with your boyfriend. It's like life stopping to give us more time together. Daniel unzips his pants for a quick foot job. Raphael knocks on the passenger-side window, freaking out. "Have you seen Philly?"

No, I didn't see you run off into the woods like a madwoman.

Louis goes into town. Daniel stays in the cottage in case you come back, and Raphael borrows the neighbour's ATV to go search the woods. I get on with him. I'm scared out of my mind, Philomena. You have no idea how angry you make me.

We find you at the edge of the cliff. A fucking cliff. You're screaming, out of your mind.

"Just let me die alone. Just let me get it over with."

My god, Philly … Not for him. Please don't let it be for Jeffrey Hudon, getting married on your birthday while things are going so well for you. It doesn't matter, Philly. Jeff doesn't even care. It doesn't mean anything. *The world doesn't fucking revolve around you.*

Raphael is shaking so hard he can barely form the words. "What are you doing, Philly?"

"It wasn't ever real between us, Raph. It was a lie, a lie, just a big, fat lie."

"Come back here."

"I'm just faking being alive, you guys."

"What are you talking about?"

"I just want to be free."

"But you are."

"I just want … want to see my dad …"

"I know, Philly."

"STOP CALLING ME THAT."

"Okay. Okay, I'm stopping."

"Tell him, Tania. Tell him that I'm meant for something more … that I've always loved diamonds …"

"I'm begging you, Philomena, get away from the edge."

I blink and you disappear.

27

Saint-François-de-Laval, Christmas vacation 2018

The city's endless humming finally beat me down. I couldn't stand the carbon monoxide, my inevitably running into old one-night stands, the soulless streets in a fast-moving city.

It just happened, like magic. Raph and I got lost in the farmers' fields of Laval looking for a squash stand. When we came across the old farmhouse with the For Sale sign out front, I almost started crying. I already loved Raph's beautiful eyes and beautiful cock, but I didn't know just how amazingly prescient he could be. He had made good investments, and with my dad's meagre life insurance policy, we were able to make a down payment. We made the offer on the last weekend in November. The house was ours the following week. The previous owner's husband had just died, and she wanted to live closer to her kids.

Raphael and I find ourselves in the middle of a pastoral scene out of a painting from 1921. The farmhouse has loads of potential but is too cluttered and busy with decor trying to keep up over the past three decades. We peel back the linoleum to find the original hardwood floors. The claw-foot tub on the second floor just needs to be re-enamelled. We stop only to listen to the sound of the rain falling on the copper roof.

At the edge of the property there's a little barn that isn't used for anything, room for invention. Anything is possible in this house.

I decorate the Christmas tree in the living room while there are still boxes to unpack. Raph stuffs an enormous turkey. His parents have come down to spend the holidays with us; my mom and her new "friend" join us for supper.

I laugh, eat, hold Raphael's hand under the table. No wine on earth tastes as good as his kisses.

We spend the rest of our vacation cross-country skiing, having endless movie marathons, spending quiet mornings working on our projects. Raph works on the media platform while I go over every panel, every word, every comma, and every cross-hatch of "In Your Human Hands" with obsessive attention to detail.

Cécile Claude has questions on what my work means; I have no choice but to dive into the deep end. Why did the Creature really let the Woman into its life? Why does love end up making her sick? Every panel has to mean something to survive the editing process. The house might be bigger than the old apartment, but I'm still too shy to spread everything out in front of Raphael. I take over part of the dark, musty basement, where I use the dark surroundings to my advantage. I can't get any closer to the Kingdom of Shadows than this. When I climb out of the basement, the light and warmth of our nest warms me from the inside out.

Raph is patient, but I know that he's curious, that he wants to see my drawings and read the story. My story. I refuse nicely; I still need to keep it to myself, keep it secret a little while longer. When we make love on the living room carpet in the middle of the afternoon, the Creature and its vultures finally fade away.

I love his eyes, his words, his ambition, his obnoxious cheeriness. I love that he loves *Moulin Rouge!*; I love that he doesn't see a monster when he looks at me. I love that this *feels* like "Come What May."

Every atom of this new world is made of calm, of respect. It's crazy how much we've changed over the years. We invite some neighbours over to celebrate the new year with some fireworks. Blooms of red, blue, and green tickle my heart. Raph and I kiss in our hoodies. My big ginger with loving eyes, he's better than my dreams; he's my world.

He makes us a midnight snack, and I set up my computer in the living room so we can celebrate with Tania and Daniel, who are in South America. Despite the distance between us, Tan and I are on the same wavelength; we absolutely had to ring in the new year together. All four of us raise a glass to our health, make a list of resolutions that we obviously can't keep. There's a voice mail waiting for me on my phone.

"Happy new year, babe."

No. Please. Fuck, no.

The floor groans beneath me. The darkness reaches up for me from the Kingdom of Shadows.

28

A thousand different visitors crowd the Quebec International Book Fair. Many leaf through my graphic novel with funny looks on their faces. Those who buy it ask me for my autograph, but my hands feel numb, detached. Everyone is talking so loud. I crumble under the onslaught of direct, personal questions. Where do you get your inspiration? What does bestiality mean to you? Do you believe in God? Why the forget-me-nots at the end?

Yeah, well, I'm still asking *myself* those questions.

Cécile Claude manages the line leading to my table with a timer in hand. I sign with shapes and squiggles that belong to someone else; I pose for pictures, a lost look on my face. The cacophony of voices and this fucking lost feeling remind me that I've never really belonged. I'm a fake.

My dad once told me that I was delivered by an eastern European doctor. Ugly as sin, but incredibly skilled at emergency C-sections and delivering babies choking on their umbilical cords. Dad used to call him Mr. Clean because of his shaved head and because the operating room was completely spotless. When he held me up, I wasn't crying — I was screaming. A little monster furious at life. Mom begged Dad to make the wailing duck quiet down. "It isn't a duck, baby. It's our little girl." Mr. Clean set me down on my mother's breast; she was still woozy from the drugs. Apparently, I kept crying like that for the next three years.

Can you see me, Daddy?

Pigs, crows, snakes put their arms around me, immortalize me on their devices, buy my book. I'm untethered, falling under an unholy spell. Hidden amongst the crowd, the Creature awaits; he's here, here for me.

We gorge on one another in the hotel bed's sandpaper sheets. I cling to his body, struggle to suffer my past life away.

When his life explodes inside me, I see vultures circling in the ceiling overhead.

29

Carleton-sur-Mer, August 2019

The room is big and empty, like a hospital for ghosts. There's only Raphael, sitting next to the bed, his face buried in his hands. The TV plays nothing but ads that go completely ignored. Sebastien Strasbourg appears on the screen, trying to convince me to bank with … I don't know. He's dressed like a grown-up, rocking a baby in his arms. I fucking hate life.

My right leg is in a cast. Multiple fractures, dislocated shoulder, and a broken rib. I wanted to kill myself; all I did was dash myself to bits. The guppy is still there, a miracle that the doctors can't explain.

I eat applesauce, licking my spoon like a distracted doe. What are *you* doing, you fucking asshole? Cutting goddamn wedding cake?

Raphael spoon-feeds me. No, please don't help me. Don't be nice to me. Don't be you.

"I talked to the doctor. You're going to have to go to therapy."

"No, I don't."

"He said there are … places … therapists … who can help …"

"Fuck, Raph. I'm all right. I'm telling you."

"You tried to kill yourself, Philly. You need help."

"Shut. Up."

The night separates into all its pieces, and each one gets under my skin, under my cast. The North star stabs my eye, the sling holding my leg up to keep me from moving. Where am I right now? The machine next to me makes weird beeping noises. Is that the sound of my soul leaving my body? Daddy? Is that you hiding behind the walls? I can feel sand grinding between my bones when I close my eyes.

Morning gives little relief: I dreamed that I lost the baby. Anguish soars. The nurse smears my stomach with cold gel and looks at the monitor with a worried look.

"Part of the uterine wall has become detached. We're going to have to monitor you for bleeding for the next few days. You might have a miscarriage. I suggest that you rest as much as possible and avoid stressful situations."

As if that's possible.

Tania is colder than the saline dripping into my veins.

"Just what the fuck were you thinking?"

"Jeff was …"

"I fucking knew it. There's no point in caring for that guy, Philomena! What are you waiting for? You've got to get over him."

"He needs me, Tania. His *wife* is the problem. Give me my clothes."

"You can't leave, Philly. You can't even walk."

"It all made sense the *second* he put his hands on me, how he touched me, kissed me. He's still in love with me, Tania!"

"What are you talking about?"

"He was there, Tania. At the book fair. I recognized his cologne. He came to Quebec to see me, just for me. We danced to Pink Floyd, we made love in … somewhere, and then he was gone."

"What?"

"We're in love, and his marriage … it's that crazy bitch's fault. I have to help him get away from her."

"Philomena, that doesn't make any sense."

"You don't get it. You're not like us. No one gets how connected we are. This is all a fucking lie. Get me out of here."

Raphael stands teary eyed in the doorway, staring. His shirt is as wet as his face. "Tell me you don't actually believe that, Philly."

"She's delusional, Raph."

"I'M NOT FUCKING DELUSIONAL! He loves me, he really loves me, okay? Jeff isn't a fucking hypocrite. You, you just pretend to love, Raphael. You think you know me, but you just want to control me. You fucking knew that I was a fucking wreck. But you … you wanted to change me, make me some perfect doll in your perfect life. But I can't be perfect. Monsters with monsters, that's how it should be. Get it into your thick little head."

"What the fuck are you *talking* about?"

"I was heartless when we met, but now I'm a soulless fucking shell. You took everything away from me. You'll never understand how much I need pain, Raphael Gouin. Fucking. Never."

"Philly, look at me. This isn't your graphic novel."

"Fuck yourself."

"You're not going to end up all alone."

"Get out of my life, Raph! LEAVE! You don't even love me, not really. He does. You just need to get it into your head. And leave."

"You're really sick, Philomena …"

"Fine. I'm sick. The fucking freak is sick in the head. Then do what you gotta do, champ. They shoot horses, don't they?"

"Philly …"

"Do it, Raph. Put me down. What? You're crying? Can't do it? Don't want to put me out of my misery? Oh, that's right. You're a *nice guy*."

"Stop it …"

"You thought you were perfect, eh? You thought you were so, so nice. But you're not. It's all an act, a mask you put on to hide the fact that you're just a fucking coward."

"A coward?"

"Like all those guys my mom used to date, like Florida-Man-Jean-Paul, Raymond, Martin, like that wanker Pierre-Luc Dion, all of them! A professional disappointer!"

"Fuck you, Philomena. I've never given up on you! I was the one! I'm the one who came up to see you in Quebec. Me! Not him!"

"You don't believe me? I'm not fucking crazy. I know what really happened."

"You were with me! Me! You thought you were dying. You were having a panic attack. You told me not to let you go, and I made love to you all night. That's what happened."

I laugh my lungs out for days and days. I find new registers, new meanings of laughter. I wanted him to hit me, but I knocked the legs out from under him. He finally leaves, and Tania cries in the hallway. Finally. They're finally going to leave me alone.

Guppy won't leave me. Guppy's still hanging on. Hanging on to what? I'm twenty-nine years old, and all I have left are lies and dust.

30

The Bridge, late September 2019

Mrs. Jorish's housecoat flaps around me in the cool breeze. It's ratty, almost see-through from all the washing. It's become my shield. On the rocky shore, I try to find a reason to live, somewhere between the far-off mountains or in the scales of the fish I caught. I've been at the centre for the past three weeks. We do group therapy with other addicts, daily one-on-ones with the shrink, self-work sessions, meditation, meetings. My new therapist, Douglas, referred me here. "Psychosis is a temporary break with reality indicative of underlying mental illness such as depression. Psychosis is not a permanent condition. It can be treated, and most people go on to lead happy lives." Fantastic.

I wear a winter coat over my jacket and thick wool socks in my canvas shoes. I'm falling apart. Three weeks cut off from

Tania, Raphael, and Mom. She must be losing her mind. We love our children more than we love ourselves.

Five o'clock in the morning on May 13, sitting on the toilet, I stared down at the pregnancy test, fingers covered in pee. Nine days late, breasts hard as stone, tears falling onto the carpet. Nine days spent fantasizing that you're his, Guppy. It was his birthday. Jeffrey is thirty years old, and I can hear him whispering dark thoughts in my ear. I'll never be a good mother, a good wife. A bitch is just a bitch. I stare down at the + sign at the end of the stick.

I'm sorry I tried to snuff you out. I'm sorry I pitted your father against us. I hope I didn't break the two of you. I've been drawing nightmares on wrinkled paper. I have addictive affective disorder branded on my DNA. At least I'm not alone.

Faizah, a young Ethiopian with a model's body, just celebrated her cotton anniversary with a man who beats the shit out of her. If you can see the bruises on her blue-black skin, it's because her loving husband has really gone too far this time. Then there's James and his testicular cancer. The doctor prescribed rest and abstinence, but he can't bring himself to delete Grindr. His insides are full of cysts. And Pauline, who has become little more than an outline, shrinking deeper and deeper into her codependent relationship with her son. Faizah, Pauline, James, and all the rest trying to get better at the Bridge. Like me. This is our last chance to learn to stay alive and love without it killing us. If this doesn't work, all I have to do is jump off a cliff. Again.

Faizah and I share a room. She braids my hair every day, and I apply makeup to hide her bruises. I say no when she first asks to read my copy of *In Your Human Hands*. Too ugly. Too violent. But she keeps pushing, and I eventually give in. When she finishes reading, she bows her head and cries, and I'm so sorry.

"I knew you shouldn't have read it."

"No, Philomena. I needed that."

She teaches me how to say *love* in Amharic before shutting off the lights for the night. I whisper the word until I fall asleep. *Fik'iri.*

The psychologist's office is flooded with morning light. I don't trust her at first, Nicole with her short hair and an art deco earring in her right ear. But after a few meetings, I start opening up, and the water frothing inside me starts to spill over.

"*Happy new year, babe.* That's it. I couldn't breathe, my bones turned to mush. I erased the message, didn't answer … But something that I hadn't felt in a long time was coming back to me, a sick throbbing. I told myself that I'd get over it. I buried myself in editing my book, in work, threw myself into my relationship. I wanted to get the old feeling back so badly …"

"When you say 'old feeling back,' what do you mean?"

"I don't know. My thoughts get so dark, sometimes … The worst thing is that part of me loves it. Pain. I've been looking for that darkness since I was little … comfortably numb …"

"Did he ever try to get into contact with you after that?"

"Before the Quebec Book Fair. That was mid-April, but it was amazingly warm outside. I remember it like it was yesterday. He wrote me to congratulate me on my book … to tell me that he misses me."

"How did that make you feel?"

"Like a piece of meat. It turned me on like crazy. Like the pack leader had chosen me as his mate. I didn't reply, but I couldn't stop thinking about him. I started pulling away from Raphael. I started to fixate on Jeff, fantasizing that we would see each other, that he'd fuck me, that he'd hurt me … It got so bad that I was getting off in the Memorium bathrooms on all my breaks to the thought of him. After … I kind of … disconnected from reality … I was delusional for four months, Nicole. All alone. In my head."

She suggests that I write a letter, to anyone I want, to get it all out. I don't want to, but I'll do it, anyway.

> *Dear Creature,*
> *You are violent and cruel, but the darkness inside*
> *you carries its own share of light, of life. My life.*
> *So, I need you. Don't be afraid. Let the light grow*
> *into the darkness. I promise I won't let it hurt you.*
> *It'll help you fly. I promise I'll never forget you. You*
> *belong inside me. You make me real, alive.*
>
> *But, I'm begging you, you have to let us keep stay-*
> *ing alive.*
>
> *Philomena, half of you, your other half.*

31

The Bridge, October 2019

I get visitors for the first time in the two months I've been here. Her red hair lights up the hallway, smelling clean and freshly washed in coconut shampoo. I bury myself in Tania's hair; mine is so ugly, I look like an overworked housewife.

"Come on, you've never been prettier, Philly. Look at your skin. You're glowing, girl. I'm almost jealous. I want to get all pregnant and glowy, too."

She has brought me a magazine with an editorial full of praise for *In Your Human Hands*. Apparently, it's the perfect graphic novel for a foggy fall afternoon. "Dark and violent but with a touch of vulnerability that shines with hope." I have to bite my cheeks to keep myself from crying. I'm going to make us some tea. Yeah, that's a good idea. A nice

verbena-mint tea to warm us up. Tania holds me tight, rub-
bing my growing belly.

"You're an inspiration, Philly."

"What do you mean?"

"You're really trying. You're here, giving yourself a chance …
I mean, we had been losing you for a while — for years — there.
And … I wasn't judging you … no. No way. It's just that … I
really freaked out in Gaspésie. I was sure you were going to …
Anyway, Dan and I have started couples' counselling."

"Yeah? Why?"

"Because we love each other, but we still have a hard time
saying it."

*And your suicide attempt hit us like a dump truck. You're not
the only one who has something to hold on to.*

"You're really an exceptional woman, Tania."

"Whoa, come on …"

"No. Really. Guppy is going to have the best godmother in
the world."

Cue Tania, screaming with joy.

We take our shoes off and put our bare feet in the little rect-
angle of light at the foot of the couch. We warm our toes, exactly like when we were little. Tania wants to change position
but stays stuck to the leather. She makes little farting noises,
and I spit tea out my nose. It's nice to have her back.

"The shrink said that we need to find coupley things to
do that aren't all about sex, so we decided to host both our
families for Christmas and make a huge supper, put up a tree,

decorations, everything. And! My mom and dad will see each other for the first time in three years. Crazy, eh?"

"Sounds perfect."

My imaginary wedding album shivers merrily.

"Is Sylvain going to make his totally crazy, over-the-top desserts?"

"Of course! I'm already planning on fasting for a whole week before and after the holidays."

"Tania."

"I know, I know, no more bad-talking my body … You and Raph will be there. It'll be so much fun! I mean, you know …"

"If we're still together?"

"If you guys don't drive up to be with his family at the Lac. Is what I meant."

Sadness crushes my intestines, and my tonsils burn in my throat. He's going to leave me; he's absolutely going to leave me. He hasn't tried to call me, to see me. If I were him, *I'd* leave me. The pain in my chest gets so bad, the guilt hollowing out my insides, that all I want to do is put my fist through a window and stick the shards of glass in my hand, my forearm, anywhere just to be able to cut out the pain stabbing me in my heart. But, no. Cutting myself won't bring him back. Breathe in. Breathe out. And accept that what you can't control is out of your hands.

"Does he at least know that I'm here?"

"Yes."

"Did he say anything?"

Tania hands me a postcard, sent from Argentina, more vibrant than ever. She turns her eyes away, lets me hold it lovingly to my chest. Behind the picture of La Boca, Raphael wrote three words. Just three.

Come what may.

32

Saint-François-de-Laval, Halloween 2019

Last day of therapy. Faizah and I have promised to help each other, to go to meetings together. To call each other if we start looking for high-up places where we can hang some rope.

Tania drives me back home. The streets are full of monsters, and I find that comforting. The big blue house looks like a mirage.

"Are you sure you don't want me to come in with you?"

"No, thanks. I'll be fine."

I have to take care of myself. Of us. My old Toyota is waiting for me in the driveway.

Daddy. Mrs. Jorish. I'm scared. Help me.

Nothing's changed, as if time hasn't ticked a second since August. And he's there. Two and a half months without seeing each other, without talking. Two months that he must have spent hating me in silence.

He got a tan in South America; his hair is longer, and his smile is just as true and real as ever. There isn't even a drop of anger or resentment in his eyes. His neck smells like pumpkin.

"I saw your waterfalls. You were right."

"I told you there's nothing more beautiful than Iguaçu."

"I can think of one."

He puts his hand on my baby bump. Please tell me I haven't done something unforgivable.

"Over here. I want to show you something."

He's worked on the abandoned little barn, turned it into a work studio. He's put in insulation, electricity, and a big old wooden table and chair on a huge berber carpet. It looks like Frida Kahlo's workshop.

"It's yours, if you want."

"For me?"

"If you want. You could use it to write, paint, create. A room of your own."

This is the last thing I could have expected.

"The Creature had ravaged her and left her to die. It had destroyed the only thing that it ever loved. The Woman. The one that, despite death, wouldn't let herself die. The Creature sniffed at the forget-me-nots and, feeling a desire to destroy coming over it, cast itself out of the Kingdom of Shadows. For it was never seen again. For centuries both plants and animals flourished under the watchful gaze the Woman cast upon its secret garden."

How do we do it? How do we start over? I want to tell him that I'm never going to be perfect, that he makes me feel more human, more real. But my throat is hoarse.

His voice sounds so beautiful. "We have a lot that we have to talk about. But tonight, can we just snuggle and eat candies?"

Lying in bed, we don't fuck, we don't go down on each other, he doesn't smack me around. We watch a movie about witches, holding each other tight. Guppy makes waves of joy in my belly.

Epilogue

Tree of Hope, Remain Strong

A Sunday night in autumn. The bare tree branches writhe like ghosts, and the lake is slowly growing winter ice. A wood-fired stove glows contentedly. Alice sleeps peacefully in her big girl bed, left leg sticking out of her sleeping bag like a crab leg. I kiss her red hair and close the bedroom door, making sure to leave a crack open because she's scared of the dark, too.

The balcony's new wood is slick under my cold bare feet. I should have put shoes on, but I never get tired of this feeling. We all rebuilt it together. Raphael and his brother Phil, Tania, Daniel, Louis, and even Sylvain came to start over from scratch.

I look up at the starry sky until I realize I'm looking for Dad up there.

Flynn Lake and its countless fish. The forest, thick with stories of ogres and warriors. The small cottage my family's been coming back to for years. We're going back tomorrow; the girls-only getaway is almost over. Tomorrow Alice and I are going back to Raphael and his golden eyes. Raphael.

"I'm no saint, Philly. I was arrogant enough to think I could save you. Can you forgive me?"

The sky is big and dark and full of dreams. Does every star shine for a broken heart?

"Mommy?"

My little three-and-a-half-year-old mouse has snuck out of bed to look for me, her face peeking through the slats on the loft guardrail. She had a bad dream, the one with the evil witch with rotten teeth. I bring her down to the stove, and she snuggles against me on the big sofa.

"Mommy has nightmares, too, sometimes. It's normal. Everyone has little monsters running around inside their heads. When I get really scared, do you know what I do? I talk to the monsters. No, really. I say, 'Hey! You can stick around, but if you scare me too much, I'm going to open my eyes and bye-bye. You'll disappear in the light.' It really works. And even if they come back from time to time, nightmares don't last forever, baby. Mommy's always going to be there."

Curled against me, she falls right back asleep.

About the Author

Eve Lemieux is a comedian, actor, and writer. *Like Animals* is her debut novel, inspired by people who haven't learned to love gently. Eve lives in Montreal.